Ms. Jane Carlton was definitely off-limits.

Wyatt felt as if someone had installed a giant neon *Trouble* sign in his apartment when he wasn't looking, and that it had just flickered on and was blinking in a fire-engine red color.

So what if she smelled really good? And had the sweetest, gentlest touch in a little spitfire of a body? Which he suspected no man had ever properly awakened before. Surely he was capable of exercising some kind of discipline where a woman was concerned.

She put the ice pack aside and came up with some kind of ointment, which she then spread very carefully with her fingertips along his eyelid, his brow and the side of his face. As she got closer and concentrated harder on getting it in exactly the right place, he shifted his weight, thinking to ease away from her. Instead, he set her off balance and her whole body fell against his. No question now. Those were her breasts pressed against him, her neck and her sweet, sassy mouth right at the corner of his own.

She gasped in surprise, her eyes suddenly all big and round.

Trouble, trouble, trouble!

Dear Reader,

Writers will tell you story ideas are all around us, and they truly are.

This idea came from a newspaper story about two elderly residents of a retirement home falling in love, much to the outrage of their respective families. Love in the eighties took on a whole new twist.

I took that idea and played with it, twisted it this way and that, turned it just so. It's what writers do to make a story our own.

Who were these people who fell in love? What were they like? What reasons would their respective families have to be upset about that? How complicated could I make this? How much fun could we all have along the way?

The result is the kind of life in our eighties and even nineties that I hope all of us have: busy, fun, active, surrounded by friends and lots of love, along with glorious adventures. (And maybe a little scheming and meddling in our loved ones' lives.)

Happy reading,

Teresa Hill

RUNAWAY VEGAS BRIDE

TERESA HILL

Silhouette

SPECIAL EDITION

Published by Silhouette Books

America's Publisher of Contemporary Romance

 **SILHOUETTE BOOKS**

ISBN-13: 978-0-373-65516-8

RUNAWAY VEGAS BRIDE

Recycling programs
for this product may
not exist in your area.

TERESA HILL

lives within sight of the mountains in upstate South Carolina with one husband, very understanding and supportive; one daughter, who's taken up drumming (earplugs really don't work that well. Neither do sound-muffling drum pads. Don't believe anyone who says they do.); and one son, who's studying the completely incomprehensible subject of chemical engineering (Flow rates, Mom. It's all about flow rates.).

In search of company while she writes away her days in her office, she has so far accumulated two beautiful, spoiled dogs and three cats (a black panther/champion hunter, a giant powder puff and a tiny tiger-stripe), all of whom take turns being stretched out, belly up on the floor beside her, begging for attention as she sits at her computer.

To my son, John,
on the occasion of his 21st birthday
and first trip to Vegas.
May your math skills and all those poker probabilities
you memorized serve you well.
And please stay far, far away from
the Love Me Tender Wedding Chapel.

Chapter One

"Darling, I'm in love!"

Jane Carlton choked on her hot tea, then covered the phone with her hand and mouthed to her assistant, "Did you say this is my grandmother?"

Lainie nodded, looking concerned. "What is it? She sounded okay. Is she okay?"

Jane threw up her hands as if to say she had no idea, then tucked the phone into her shoulder once again and said, "Gram?"

"Yes, dear. Did you hear me?"

"I...maybe," Jane admitted. "Say it again?"

"I'm in love!"

The words came out sounding like lyrics in a musical—theatrical, whimsical, larger-than-life.

There was just one problem.

The women in Jane's family didn't do love. They didn't do forevers.

Oh, they had men in their lives. But they made no mistakes about it involving anything as substantial and long-lasting as love.

Jane had learned that the hard way.

"Gram, I thought—"

"I know. I know! That's why it's so amazing! Me, in love, finally, at seventy-six! Who'd have believed it?"

"Wait," Jane said, shaking her head. "Gram, you're eighty-one—"

"He moved into one of the cottages a week ago! The most amazing man I've ever met in my life, Jane, and… Oh, here he comes! Leo! Over here! Over here!"

Jane's grandma sounded like a teenager.

This was so bizarre.

Was it some kind of sudden-onset dementia that had her believing she was only seventy-six? Worst yet, could that have taken her back in her own mind to her teenage years in the four days since Jane's last visit?

Because that's what she sounded like, a ridiculous kid in love.

"Say you'll come and have dinner with us so you can meet him," Gram said. "Tonight? All right? It's lasagna night. Goodbye, my darling girl."

Thursdays.

Lasagna night.

One of Jane's big dates of the week.

Thursdays was lasagna with Gram, her great-aunt Gladdy and a few of their friends from their active retirement village—they stressed the word *active* in all things—called Remington Park. Sunday afternoons were spent taking Gram and Gladdy shopping, maybe to a movie or brunch.

There it was, the sad truth about Jane's big dates.

Oh, she could have found a man to go out with. Men were everywhere. But a man she truly wanted to spend time with? A man who could be depended on to show her a good time that topped a hot bath, a glass of wine and a good book?

There certainly weren't a lot of those around, Jane had found in her twenty-eight years.

She put down the phone—forgotten by Gram, who'd gone in search of Leo, the supposed love of her life—and sighed, trying not to think Gram had more of a social life than she did.

"Is she all right?" Lainie asked, hovering as she tended to do.

"Well, she's either forgotten her own age or she's pretending to be five years younger to impress a man. Please tell me we won't give a flip about impressing a man when we're eighty-one. I mean, at that age, who really wants one? They're bound to be more trouble than they're worth in their eighties. I mean, I think men in their thirties are more trouble than they're worth."

Lainie frowned. "Jane, you think all men are more trouble than they're worth."

Jane considered, decided she couldn't argue that point. "And?"

Lainie looked sad, as if she might just feel a bit sorry for Jane. "I'm just saying… Don't you ever get lonely?"

Absently drumming the keys on the powered-off calculator on her desk, Jane considered. "Not really. I have my work, my family. I guess I'm a little lonely now that Bella's gone—"

"Bella was a dog, Jane."

"I know. I've never met a man who was nicer to me than my dog was."

Then there was no even trying to hide it. Lainie definitely felt sorry for her, which made Jane wonder if it was really that sad, to have a beloved and recently deceased dog who was nicer to her than any man she'd ever met. But really, Jane felt lucky to have no illusions. To be honest with herself and in the way she'd put together a life of her choosing. And it was a good life. A good, satisfying life most of the time.

Sure, every now and then she got lonely, but didn't everyone?

"Men are so unpredictable," she complained.

"Life is unpredictable," Lainie insisted.

"No, life with men is unpredictable." Jane smiled, quite satisfied with that catchphrase.

She quickly scribbled it down on a list she kept handy for just these occasions. She'd come up with another great catchphrase for her work with the poor, unhappy women who hadn't yet come to the wisdom she had, wisdom she happily shared with others in her Fabulous Female Financial Boot Camp seminars. Where she preached financial independence with the same fervor of a good old-fashioned preacher trying to save lost souls. The women in her seminars were lost, too, in a wilderness of financial ignorance, irresponsibility and the completely mistaken idea that they were helpless to assist themselves, to take control of their own financial destiny.

Men were what messed up everything.

Most women would be so much better off without them.

Jane didn't come right out and say that, exactly, to the

poor, lost female souls who came to her. She didn't want to freak them out too badly right away, and Jane knew she could really freak people out if she wasn't careful, being so passionate and insistent in getting her ideals across. She just told women that unless and until they were in charge of their own lives, they would never have any true independence or stability, and that who, if anyone, should be in charge of their lives except themselves?

Empowerment and enlightenment, Jane promised in the advertisements for her seminars. *Changing women's lives for the better.*

Jane was completely in charge of her own life, and it was wonderfully predictable, dependable and sane.

And she liked it that way.

Wyatt Addison Gray IV got *the look* the minute he walked in the door at the main offices of Remington Park.

The administrator, a most aptly named Ms. Steele, was waiting for him, all starched and pressed and so buttoned-up it looked like her blouse might be strangling her, even as she stood there.

Wyatt asked himself, How bad could it possibly be? The man had only been here for a week. How much havoc could an eighty-six-year-old man possibly cause in seven days?

And come to think of it, why couldn't his uncle be immobile like so many men his age? Maybe just stuck in a wheelchair that conveniently didn't move, the wheels sabotaged for his own good? Was that too much to ask? Drugged into a mild haze that left him feeling no pain and causing no trouble? What would it take to arrange that? It wasn't really illegal, was it? Drugging and restraining a troublesome eighty-six-year-old?

Wyatt tried to fortify himself for what was to come, put on his best I-can-fix-this smile and extended a hand. "Ms. Steele. What can I do for you?"

"You promised there wouldn't be any trouble," she said, attacking from the first word as she stood in the doorway to her office.

"Yes," he said, pretending he believed every word he was about to say.

No trouble.

No problem.

Nothing to fix.

She gave a curt nod that said, *Inside my office. Now.*

Wyatt smiled reassuringly and then tried to appear calm and confident—none of which he felt—as he complied with her unspoken command.

Ms. Steele seated herself behind a desk organized with rigid precision, pen here, clock here, phone here, files neatly housed in a small holder on her desk, paper in a short stack that looked like someone had taken a ruler to the edges.

Ooh, Wyatt thought, feeling like he was a teenager and had been summoned to the headmaster's office at boarding school. *Again.*

He sat back, determined to at least seem relaxed, and smiled. "What can I do for you?"

She huffed like she was already disgusted with him and his uncle, and Wyatt hadn't even begun to make his explanations yet.

"You think those of us in the eldercare community don't know each other?" she began. "Don't talk? Don't get together to share our problems and ideas on how to address them?"

Oh, hell.

He hoped not. Though he probably should have thought

of that and negotiated a confidentiality clause with the other retirement homes his uncle had been in.

"Well, we do talk to each other," Ms. Steele said. "And I did some checking. I don't know how I let you talk me into taking him without talking to some people first—"

Wyatt knew exactly how he'd done it. It was, simply, what he did—talk people into things they didn't want to do. He was a divorce lawyer, and what he'd found, mostly, was that by the time they got to him, people really didn't want to divorce their spouse. They wanted to torture their spouse, mercilessly and without end, and the way to do that was to keep fighting about the divorce.

So he usually let them fight it out for a while, chalking up billable hours like crazy, until most of the fury had burned out, that gleam in their eyes about revenge giving way to exhaustion and growing financial distress, and then he talked them into what they really needed to do. Agree to the divorce.

It sounded cold and maybe a little as if he was taking advantage, but truly, he wasn't. People needed that time to let their emotions rage, he'd discovered. It wasn't pretty, but it was all about processing those bad, messy feelings that came from the breakup of most relationships. And without that processing time, people simply couldn't move on.

He gave them that time, at an outrageous sum per hour, as most attorneys did, and then when he felt they were ready, he got them to agree to the actual divorce.

Wyatt liked to think he provided a much-needed service to the miserably married public, that he gave his clients a nice balance of hand-holding, emotional venting opportunities and, in the end, closure. For that, he was incredibly well paid and had learned how to talk almost anyone into anything. A skill that he never imagined he'd need in such abundance in looking after his beloved but troublesome elderly uncle in the man's waning years.

Problem was, certain things about uncle Leo showed no signs of waning. Most distressingly, his interest in women.

When they'd come to Remington Park, Wyatt had been at his most charming, most reassuring, pushing to seal the deal without ever seeming like he was pushing, seeming like a man with no troubles at all, when he convinced Ms. Steele to take uncle Leo.

"Kicked out of three retirement homes already!" Ms. Steele commented.

It wasn't a question. She knew it was true. *Damn.* "Look, he just went a little…you know—"

"No, I don't," Ms. Steele said. "The man's eighty-six, not sixteen!"

"He and my aunt Millicent were together for eleven years," Wyatt explained.

Ms. Steele didn't seem impressed at all with the number.

Wyatt frowned. "No one in my family's ever stayed married that long. This was the marathon of marriages for the Gray family men—a record likely to stand for the ages if history is any guide—and uncle Leo was faithful to her the entire time. He swears it. But then, when she was gone… I mean, he was devastated. Truly, he was. But he also felt like…"

"He was running out of time?" she suggested.

Wyatt nodded. "I suppose."

"Had to get everything while he still could?"

That sounded more selfish than he'd ever considered Leo to be, but still, Wyatt conceded, "It's possible."

"A little like a kid in a candy store, given the fact that there are so many more women than men at his age? Or even in the age group ten or twenty years younger than he is? So many lonely women with no one to talk to? No one to flatter them? Flirt with them? Hold them? Convince them to let him take care of certain physical needs they might have forgotten, that he can bring back to life, like magic?"

"Okay, yes. He likes women," Wyatt admitted. "Always has. And they like him."

"Don't expect me to see this as some sort of public service he's offering. Servicing—if you will—lonely women," she said, looking every bit as dour and imposing as the last administrator who'd kicked uncle Leo out of her facility. "Because I certainly don't see it that way."

"And how do you see it?" Wyatt asked, thinking if he knew where she was coming from, surely he could fix this.

"Like he has caused women who've lived together happily, some of them for years in the same cottage, to now be at each other's throats! Like they were in high school, fighting over a boy! I won't have it. I can't—"

"Look, he's a flirt—"

She frowned down her upturned nose, holding a file folder in front of her. "He's doing more than flirting."

Damn, Wyatt thought. Leo's still got it. At eighty-six! A part of him couldn't help but feel a sense of admiration and reassurance about his own twilight years.

Eighty-six and still going.

On the other hand, he could really go for Leo moderately drugged and confined to a deliberately sabotaged wheelchair in an all-male home right now.

Did they have those? All-male homes? Wyatt would have to look into it, if he couldn't salvage this situation.

"Look, these women… He swears he doesn't make them any promises. No commitments. I told him he had to make that clear up front, so no one would get hurt." He'd thought about actually drafting a release, spelling it out in writing. No expectations of any permanent arrangement. And getting them all to sign before Leo got too close. "I mean, surely women still aren't looking for a long-term commitment in their eighties? Please tell me they're not?"

Ms. Steele looked aghast.

"He can't help it if women like him," Wyatt said.

"The women here got along just fine with each other until he came," Ms. Steele reiterated. "So I don't think the women are the problem. He is. And if he causes any more of an uproar here, he's gone. I mean it. And you'll have to take him out of state to find him a new home. I won't have him doing the same thing to anyone I know in this business."

Okay, so…it wasn't that bad yet? They still had a chance. What a relief!

"He'll be great," Wyatt vowed. "Quiet, kind—without being too kind. Friendly without being too friendly. A model resident. I promise."

Bigger lies had seldom fallen from Wyatt's lips, he feared.

He wrapped up his meeting with Ms. Steele and went to find his uncle.

Remington Park was actually a series of small cottages, each housing eight to ten residents who had their own bedrooms and shared a common kitchen, living room and dining room. Those cottages were set around larger, more traditional assisted living apartments and a nursing home facility for people who needed a higher level of care. Once they could no longer live in the cottages comfortably, they could move next door to assisted living or the nursing home, without leaving all the friends they'd made within the community.

The whole complex also had extensive walking trails, gardens, a few small shops, a pool, a rehab center and cafeteria, and boasted of the fitness and activity level of its residents.

Wyatt thought it seemed homey, those little cottages— kind of like old-fashioned boarding houses. Plus there were the more traditional care options. He hadn't thought, as he clearly should have, that with the place being this big, there were bound to be tons of women.

As he walked down the path that led to Leo's cottage, he saw them. Some of them frail-looking and hunched over, some of them glossy, white-haired, beauties-in-their-day women, bare arms pumping with each step, wearing walking shorts, their toned, tanned legs moving at a pace that might even leave Wyatt breathless as they went about their exercise.

As Leo liked to say, eighty was the new sixty.

Wyatt just shook his head and thought he had to get to the gym more. He could take out some of his frustrations over Leo there, and he wanted to be in good shape, still able to chase women if he wanted to when he was in his eighties.

He got to Leo's cottage, then to Leo's room, but seeing it was empty, went to the kitchen and asked the young woman in the cheery yellow polo shirt the staff wore where his uncle was. But she wasn't sure.

"He doesn't spend much time in his room," she said, looking like she was trying to be diplomatic and maybe was a little scared.

Wyatt wondered if she was the one who had squealed on Leo to the dragon-lady administrator. Poor girl. She didn't look like she was much past twenty and certainly no match for Leo at his most charming or most manipulative.

"Do you have any idea where he spends most of his time, if not in his room?" Wyatt tried.

"Well, he has a new lady friend," she admitted. "I mean…at least one new one that I know of. It's hard to keep up, you know?"

"I know," Wyatt admitted.

"There's a bench on a little hill in the formal gardens overlooking the outdoor pool. You know where the outdoor pool is?"

Wyatt nodded, remembering from the tour.

"I've heard him say how much he likes that spot." She leaned in closer, whispering. "The view…of the ladies at the pool, sunbathing… You know what I mean?"

"Oh, yes."

Bathing beauties had always done it for the Gray men.

"You might try there," she offered.

Wyatt thanked her.

He found the gardens, followed the sound of low laughter and a faint blend of '40s big-band music to the little hill overlooking the outdoor pool.

There was the bench, but no Leo.

Then Wyatt heard giggling.

Leo had always had a knack for making the women laugh.

Around a bush, a cypress tree and a decorative rock wall, there was a more secluded bench and Leo with his arms around a lovely white-haired woman, her head laid back against his arm as she gazed up at him adoringly. He bent down to kiss her, his hands starting to wander.

"Leo," she said, still giggly, pushing one wandering hand away. "We just met!"

Wyatt rolled his eyes and swore under his breath.

Leo copping a feel at eighty-six, just like a damn teenage boy with more hormones than functioning brain cells.

Was there some sort of anti-Viagra? Something they could slip into Leo's nightly bourbon and Coke? Maybe that would do the trick.

Wyatt strode forward, calling out to his uncle as he did. The lady jumped up and away from Leo, blushing like an innocent young miss.

Leo got to his feet, too, smiling for all he was worth. "Wyatt, my boy. What are you doing here?"

"Oh, I think you know," Wyatt said.

Chapter Two

Leo introduced his lady-friend, Kathleen, who shook Wyatt's hand and said, "Leo's told me all about you. He just adores you."

Wyatt smiled as best he could, put an arm around Leo's shoulder that left no doubt Leo was to stay right there. "Leo's a real character, isn't he?"

"I hope you'll be joining us for dinner," Kathleen added. "It's lasagna night, and we could all get to know each other better."

"Mmm," Wyatt said, making no promises.

Although maybe he could prevent a fight from breaking out over dinner, if he stayed. Leo had a bad habit of inviting more than one woman to share the same meal with him. It wasn't a forgetfulness-that-comes-with-age thing, either. He'd been double-booking himself for decades.

"Well," Kathleen said, looking from Wyatt to Leo and then

back to Wyatt again. "I suppose you two could use some time to catch up. Leo, I'll see you at six o'clock at my cottage. Don't you forget this time or I'll have to come find you."

She gave him a kiss on the cheek and then walked away.

Leo watched her go, trim, toned legs in neat, short socks and sneakers. He'd always been a leg man.

Wyatt just shook his head. "For a woman you just met, she sounds a tad possessive. She's ready to hunt you down if you don't show up on time for dinner."

"Damn, that's a pretty woman. You should see her in a bathing suit," Leo confided, shaking his head appreciatively. "Seventy-six, and she's still got it."

"She's lovely," Wyatt agreed.

"Kind of reminds me of your father's third wife. What was her name? Elaine?"

"No, Elaine was number four. I can't remember number three's name at the moment. She was the one who only lasted a few months. I was at boarding school practically the whole time."

"Oh, yeah. The redhead. I'd forgotten about her," Leo said, then had the grace to look a bit sorry. "So, the Dragon Lady summoned you, boy?"

Wyatt nodded. "And it only took a week. That's a record, Leo."

"Yeah, that woman really needs a good man to loosen her up, make her smile once in a while, you know?"

Wyatt rolled his eyes. "Don't tell me you're going to fix everything by taking the Dragon Lady out for a spin, so to speak?"

"No, no, no. Not me! I'm just saying, a good roll in the sack would do wonders for her."

Wyatt sat down on the bench and buried his face in his

hands. The men in his family tended to think good sex fixed everything, when it was usually the beginning of all their problems. How could they not know this by now? Especially at Leo's age?

"I'm not here to talk about the Dragon Lady's sex life or lack of a sex life."

"Yeah, yeah. I know," Leo grumbled. "Bunch of damn uptight prudes! They expect a man's life to be over at my age. Well, I'm tellin' you, boy. Leonardo Gray's life is far from over! And I intend to enjoy every last minute of it."

"Well, if you want to enjoy it here—" Wyatt began.

"I do. I like it here. Beautiful women all over the place. Women who really know how to take care of themselves, too. Did you get a good look at my Kathleen? Great legs."

"Yes, she has gorgeous legs," Wyatt agreed. "And if you want to be here to admire them, you've got to tone down the charm, Leo. The flirting with everyone you see. You know how women get their hopes up when you're around. They tend to always think you're offering them more than you are. Things more permanent than you want."

Leo made a disgusted sound. "Permanent? What the hell is permanent when you're eighty-one—"

"You're eighty-six, Leo."

"I know that! Don't you think I know that! But I can't be saying it all the time. Otherwise, I might forget and say it in front of the women. They get a little squirrelly at the idea of a man not that far from ninety. Not that I'm scared of it. Hell, it's just a number. If I'm still around, I'll still have it when I'm ninety. You wait and see!"

Wyatt just groaned at the idea of Leo the Ladies Man, still havin' it at ninety.

* * *

Jane arrived promptly at five minutes to six.

She prided herself at being on time, always, which she accomplished by consistently being five minutes early for any appointment. Being on time was a mark of respect for others and a sign of good organizational skills, she thought, both virtues Jane strived to portray to the world at large.

She walked into the cottage Gram and Aunt Gladdy shared with four other women, all friends from childhood who'd grown up together in Maryland and even if they'd moved away at times, came back home in their later years.

Gram could have lived independently, but she and Gladdy had shared a house off and on for sixty years. In fact, the first apartment they'd ever lived in on their own had been in the same boarding house. They were both attending secretarial school in hopes of snagging their rich bosses as husbands, something they both had managed to do, although neither one's marriage had lasted long. They happily moved in together again and again, as various entanglements with men began and inevitably went bad over the years.

When Gladdy broke her hip a year ago and was facing a couple of months in rehab, maybe more, Gram missed Gladdy so much, she moved into Remington Park with her. Once there, they found so many old friends in residence, they didn't want to leave. Gram said it was like being back in the boarding house and twenty-one all over again. It was the homeyness of that little eight-person cottage that did it, that and all the activities.

Gram said she hadn't realized how much fun it was to have people around all the time and to have so many things to do, right there where they lived. She and Gladdy had always been social creatures, and as long as they were happy, Jane was happy.

She'd never expected anything like Gram falling in love.

Jane said hello to Gram's friend Ms. Bea, who was knitting in her favorite chair in the corner of the living room, and Alice, who was heading for the door in a terry cloth swimsuit cover-up, blowing kisses at Jane as she went.

The cottages' favorite aide, Amy, was in the dining room setting the table. Amy was twenty-one and had a five-year-old of her own, Max, who all the ladies of the cottage adored and secretly looked after on days when Max didn't have kindergarten or Amy's babysitter was a no-show.

"Hi, Amy. Dinner smells delicious," Jane said, putting a bakery box on the counter. "I brought cupcakes for everyone, including you and Max."

Amy beamed at her, grateful for every little thing anyone did for her and her son. "Jane, you spoil us."

"And you spoil everyone here, so we're far from even. But I have to try," Jane said, more grateful than she could ever express to know that Gram and Gladdy were so well taken care of and happy here. "So, given any thought to my offer to help get your application together for the culinary arts institute?"

Amy made a face. "I told you, this is the best job I've ever had. These ladies are sweet and happy almost all the time, and they take care of me and Max as much as I take care of them. I worked a lot harder than this at home when I was twelve taking care of my younger brothers and sisters for free. This is a piece of cake."

"But you're such a wonderful cook—"

"And I cook here, and people love my food," she reasoned.

"But, I know the pay for aides in a retirement community is not good." Abysmal, actually. How could any woman live on that, and the workers here were primarily female, as the lowest-paid workers most usually were, Jane knew.

"Yes," Amy admitted. "But all I have is my GED. You don't make a lot of money with a GED."

"Which is why going back to school is so important," Jane said.

"And costs a ton of money. Where would I get the money?"

"There are programs to loan money to people who are furthering their education. I'll bring the paperwork here. We can fill it out together."

"And then what? Classes at night? Working all day? When am I going to see Max? I'm all he has. And I can't afford to pay someone to take care of him all the time." Amy looked tired suddenly, taking care of too many people for too long with no one to help her.

"Do it now, and you'll be grateful for the rest of your life and Max's. No more living paycheck to paycheck. Think about it. Job security, health insurance. You can do it. I know you can," Jane promised, trying not to break into her basic speech on education and financial well-being with all the bells and whistles, the cheerleading, the chants, the whole bit.

She tended to do that, even when she wasn't on the podium conducting a seminar, and it made some people uncomfortable.

"I'll think about it," Amy said. "But I just don't see how I can make it work."

"I do. I've helped thousands of women just like you get back to school and get good jobs—"

"Jane?" Gram said, as she and Gladdy came around the

corner and into the kitchen. "Don't nag, dear. Amy loves it here, and we can't imagine this place without her."

"Sorry, Amy." Jane took a breath and hoped she truly did look sorry.

Gram thought Jane was too militant in her ways, crusading for women's financial freedom and security.

Of course, Gram and Gladdy's idea of financial security was a man, a well-to-do man. Jane had finally convinced them to at least ask for gold and diamonds as gifts from their various admirers. Gold and diamonds held their value quite well and could always be sold, if need be. Stock certificates and bonds in divorce settlements worked well, too. They'd been involved with enough men, by this age, to have accumulated smartly diverse and extensive investment portfolios, something of which Jane, who'd handled their finances for years, was very proud.

"Don't worry." Amy laid her hand on top of Jane's. "It's fine. And it's nice to have someone who cares."

"I do," Jane promised. "If you ever decide to leave here, or they catch you bringing Max to work one day, promise to call me."

"Jane!" Gram said again.

"You know the administrator would fire Amy if she ever caught Max here during Amy's working hours," Jane argued in her own defense.

"We love Max and Amy, and we are very good at hiding Max when necessary," Aunt Gladdy said. "Plus, we have our eyes out for a nice young man for Amy. We're going to find her someone fabulous!"

Jane groaned, then looked pleadingly at Amy. "A man is not the answer."

"They are to some things," Amy countered. "I've been alone a long time, if you know what I mean."

"Okay, men have their uses," Jane admitted. "Limited at best, but they are not the answer."

"Well, I don't know about that," a lively older man claimed, smiling as he took his place by Gram's side and leaned over to give her a little kiss on the cheek. "I'd have to say it depends on exactly what the question is."

Though he looked younger, Jane would bet money he was at least eighty, maybe older, just because she knew men seemed to think they were entitled to a younger woman, the younger the better.

Her father had already married and divorced two women younger than Jane. Why was that, exactly, that they thought they were entitled to younger and younger women? Didn't they know how ridiculous they looked? Running around with wives younger than their daughters?

Jane had never been able to figure that one out.

And she feared she disliked Leo Gray on sight.

Gram gave him a dazzling smile, which faded fast after Leo greeted her and then turned to give Gladdy the same treatment, little kiss on the cheek and all. Gladdy glowed for a moment, then caught Gram's look and eased maybe an inch farther away from Leo.

So… Gladdy liked him, too?

Not good, Jane thought. Really not good.

She tried to comfort herself by remembering that in all their years together, Gram and Gladdy had never fought over a man. Surely they wouldn't start now.

Gram put her hand on Leo's arm and said, "Leo Gray, meet my favorite granddaughter, Jane Clayton. Jane, darling, this is Leo."

Jane held out her hand, only to find Leo clasping it in both of his and slowly bringing it to his lips for the barest hint of a kiss. "Well, she is just as adorable as you said, Kathleen. I can see now what you must have looked like as a girl, you gorgeous thing."

Adorable?

Girl?

He made it sound like Jane was six. She fumed but said nothing, not wanting to embarrass Gram.

This was going to be a very long dinner.

"Men have their uses. Limited at best…"

Wyatt caught that much as he followed Leo through the cottage door, then hung back, not wanting to walk into the middle of that particular conversation. Leo, of course, had no reservations about getting into anything with any number of women, kissing his new lady-love, Kathleen, and her friend, which Wyatt could see didn't go over so well with Kathleen.

Jeez, right in front of her like that? What was Leo thinking?

And the granddaughter, Jane, the *adorable girl,* had just met Leo and already she was fuming on her grandmother's behalf.

Wyatt decided navigating this room was going to take all the diplomatic skills he possessed, that he'd rather step in between feuding spouses on the way to divorce court than this particular group.

Bracing himself, he walked to Leo's side.

"My nephew Wyatt dropped by for a few minutes. To take care of some business for me," Leo said. "He met Kathleen in the garden by the pool earlier. Gladdy, my dear, Jane, meet Wyatt. Wyatt, these two lovely ladies are Kathleen's cousin Gladdy and her granddaughter, Jane."

Wyatt smiled and nodded to Gladdy, a shorter, more gently rounded version of Kathleen with the same pretty white hair. He would have done the same to Jane, but she stood ramrod straight and extended a hand, giving him a firm, businesslike handshake, which he returned in the same manner, fighting the urge to snap to attention and salute at the way she held herself.

He hoped he passed her little test, being properly businesslike and not trying the bowing-over-the-back-of-the-hand kiss Leo favored in greeting all women, whether they were five or one hundred and five.

Wyatt anticipated Jane might have slapped him if he'd tried it. He'd seen her reaction to Leo's patented move, after all.

She was obviously going for the classic power-suit look some women favored, and she might have pulled it off. She had the matching skirt and jacket in power-red, a no-frills white blouse, hair raked back from her face in a severe knot and carried her leather briefcase by her side.

It was just that Jane was pint-size, maybe five foot two, Wyatt guessed.

She looked like a dress-up doll in that outfit. Like a little girl who'd been sneaking into her mother's closet.

It was cute, really, if a man liked that sort of thing, though he was certain that was not the look she was going for.

His mouth twitched, amusement warring with the need not to offend her or to show any undo interest. After all, she already thought Leo was an awful flirt. Wyatt didn't want her to think all the Gray men were like that.

"Well, it was lovely to meet you all," Wyatt said. "I

won't keep you from your dinner. Leo, just don't forget what we talked about, okay?"

"Wyatt, you're not staying for dinner?" Kathleen asked.

"Oh, honey, it's my fault," Leo said. "I didn't know he was coming by today, and I didn't call in time to make a reservation for him."

Wyatt hadn't been here for dinner yet. He usually took Leo out to a restaurant nearby. But he knew guests were welcome, for a slight meal fee and with a few hours' notice, to make sure there was enough for everyone in the cottage who wanted to eat that evening.

"Sorry, ladies. Another time," he responded, thinking how happy he was to escape this little group.

"Oh, you're welcome to stay," Amy piped up from the kitchen. "We have a resident who has a sore throat and just told me that she wasn't coming to dinner tonight. So there's plenty."

Wyatt tried to keep the pained expression from his face, knowing it might be smart to stay and see firsthand what the problem was, maybe even talk to Leo's new lady himself and set her straight about Leo's abysmal record with women, much as he dreaded the idea.

"Well, in that case, I'd be happy to join you," he said.

Leo held out a chair for Kathleen, and Wyatt did the same for Gladdy, then hesitated over doing so for Jane, feeling she would see it as an insult to her abilities to pull out her own chair, rather than plain, old-fashioned manners.

He played it safe and stood back, indicating that she should take her choice of seats, the one next to Gladdy or Kathleen. Leo, of course, seated himself between the two women at the small, round table. Jane picked the seat next to Gladdy, leaving Wyatt the one next to Kathleen.

Everything was fine for a while. The food was actually outstanding. He joined the others in heaping praise on the very young-looking girl who had made and served the meal.

Amy, a bit flustered by the attention, fumbled the fork on his empty plate as she removed it, and Wyatt and Jane both hurried to bend over and pick it up.

And that's when Wyatt—and unfortunately Jane—saw it.

They already knew Leo was leaning comfortably toward Kathleen, his arm stretched across the back of her chair, his hand cupping her far shoulder. But now that they'd bent over to pick up the fork, they could see he was also holding hands under the table with Gladdy! He pulled his hand away when they bent over, but not quickly enough.

Jane gave an outraged huff, her mouth falling open, eyes shooting sparks at Wyatt under the table. Wyatt, hoping he looked properly shocked to Jane, picked up the fork and slowly straightened.

He handed the lost fork to Amy, then got another zinging look from Jane. Gladdy, he noted, had the grace to blush and carefully bring both her hands to the top of the table, clasping them together almost in a prayer-like motion.

Begging them not to tell?

Leo, the idiot, looked relaxed as could be, and Kathleen perhaps a bit confused, but smiling all the same in that lovely way of hers.

Wyatt wiped his mouth with his cloth napkin and as unobtrusively as possible, leaned toward Jane and whispered, "Meet me at that bar across the street after this? We need to talk."

Her seething look said, *Yes, we certainly do.*

Chapter Three

"What in the world is wrong with that man?" Jane demanded, upon entering the bar, not even bothering to sit down.

Wyatt had selected a table in the far corner, wanting privacy and anticipating that this conversation might get loud at some point. Not thinking she'd walk in and stand there, all puffed up and mad, trying to glare down at him. A ridiculous attempt, given how tiny the woman was.

Even sitting down, he could very nearly look her in the eye.

And she was really adorable when she was spitting fire like that. Not that Wyatt would dare tell her. She already had a terrible opinion of the men in his family.

"Is he demented in some way that isn't quite obvious to a person untrained in geriatric medicine?" Jane asked, hands on her hips, still filled with anger.

"Unfortunately not," Wyatt told her.

"Unfortunately?" She enunciated each syllable like he might be demented himself and didn't quite understand the big word.

"Yes. If he was actually impaired in some way, he'd have some excuse for his behavior," Wyatt admitted. "Jane, I'm very sorry, but there's simply no excuse. It's just the way he is. Always has been. He's like a kid in a candy store where women are concerned."

He had her agreeing with him for a minute, maybe even sympathizing, and then she started seething again.

"Kid in a candy store? Like women are all laid out in a row, his for the taking, waiting for him to pick which one he wants?"

"Unfortunately, yes. He's just that…" Wyatt would have said confident, but stopped himself. He thought she might have hit him, if he had. "Look, I know it's…offensive, especially to someone like you—"

"Someone like me?" She practically spit the words at him.

"A modern woman," he said, trying desperately to save himself now. "An enlightened woman. A strong, successful, extremely capable woman."

Who doesn't think she needs a man for anything at all. He got it. He understood her perfectly, he believed. Oh, yes, he did, because his last words placated her a bit.

"Look, the man was born in a different era. He was raised to see women and relationships differently than we do today," Wyatt tried, not about to explain that his father, twenty years Leo's junior, thought of women the same way and that he'd been raised much in the woman-as-candy-in-a-store philosophy, too.

"That's really no excuse for his behavior," Jane said, not quite as militant-sounding as before.

"I know. Believe me, I do, and I'm sorry." Wyatt dared to pull out the seat next to him and offer it to her. "Jane, please, sit down. Let's talk about this. Let me get you a drink. God knows, I need one after dealing with Uncle Leo."

She looked a bit miffed, like she'd been winding up for a really great fight or a rant on women's rights, and he was depriving her of that opportunity by agreeing with her and apologizing. It was one of Wyatt's greatest weapons—being able to soothe outraged females. He was a master at work right now, even if he did say so himself, much like Leo in that gigantic candy store of women.

Jane sat, still looking as if she didn't trust him a bit, but not foaming at the mouth or anything. With Jane, he decided, that was progress.

He motioned for the waitress who'd been hovering a few feet away, figuring out if they were really going to start a fight at the bar and how she might handle it. She came to the table, looking a bit nervous but calming down as Jane stayed silent.

At his quiet question about her drink preference, Jane looked a bit sheepishly at the waitress and murmured, "White wine spritzer, please."

Wyatt tried to contain a grimace at the idea of wanting to dilute good wine with anything, at the idea of such a sissy, girly drink. Jane didn't seem girly at all. Maybe she didn't approve of really drinking. She was prim and buttoned-up after all.

"You're going to make fun of my drink?" she asked, apparently not going to let him get away with anything.

"I wouldn't dream of it," Wyatt insisted. Then asked for a bourbon, straight up.

Jeez, the woman was prickly.

The waitress nodded, promised to bring their drinks right away, and then escaped, looking quite happy to get far, far away from them.

Wyatt sat back in his chair, trying to look relaxed and in perfect control of the spitfire that was Jane. "So, as I said before, my uncle's attitude toward women is inexcusable. Outdated, sexist, arrogant, immature. I realize that. I freely admit it and apologize sincerely for it."

Jane gave him an odd look, hopefully discarding the next three insults she had planned to hurl at him over Leo's behavior.

Good. They were getting somewhere.

"If there was anything I could do to change the way he behaves, believe me, I would have done it years ago. It's caused him and me enormous amounts of trouble and grief. But I fear, at eighty-six—"

"Eighty-six? He told Gram he was only eighty-one."

"Well, he's not," Wyatt went on. "Honestly, a woman can't believe a word that man says, and unfortunately, I simply cannot change him. I've tried. So, at this point, all I can do is be completely up front about…how he is…and hope that saves women like your grandmother and great-aunt from being hurt by him."

"That's it? That's your solution?"

Wyatt shrugged, trying to look both reasonable and helpless at the same time. "I don't know what else to do. He's a grown man. I have virtually no control over him. Any more than you can control your grandmother—"

"My grandmother's not the one running around with two different people at the same time."

Wyatt could only pray it was merely two women for Leo at the moment.

"I was just hoping," he explained quietly, "that your grandmother might be more…reasonable…to deal with than my uncle. That once we explain to her…the way he is…"

"You want to tell her that he's a complete cad and a liar?" Jane asked.

"Better than her finding out on her own. And, actually, I thought you might tell her. That the news might be easier coming from you. But if you think it should come from me, of course, I'll do it."

Jane's mouth fell open, literally.

The waitress returned with their drinks. Jane didn't touch hers. Wyatt downed his in one long gulp.

"Another, please?" he asked the waitress before she left.

Jane leaned toward him, whispering urgently, "My grandmother thinks she's in love with him!"

Wyatt sighed, feeling a headache coming on. "He's only been there a week."

"I know. It's ridiculous, I admit, but she does! What in the world does he do to these women?"

Wyatt could only shake his head in wonder. He refrained from saying that surely any woman who could believe she was in love in a week's time was, perhaps, just asking to get hurt.

He wouldn't dare say that to Jane.

She sat back in her chair, looking sad and worried. "You have to understand, my grandmother has never been in love before. She's had men, of course. She's a beautiful woman.

Been married a number of times, and been genuinely happy for a time with a man, but she's never claimed to be in love. She doesn't even believe in love, as far as I know."

"So what the devil happened between the two of them?"

"I have no idea."

Jane sat back in her chair, taking a sip of her wine spritzer. What could this man possibly find offensive about a white wine spritzer?

But on the topic of Leo, she had to concede to herself at least, that for a man, Wyatt Gray was being exceedingly reasonable, much as she hated admitting it.

He had acknowledged his uncle's bad behavior and didn't really try to make excuses, merely admitting he was incapable of controlling the man. Jane had tried for decades to change Gram and Gladdy's attitudes toward life in general and men in particular without much success. Except for getting control of their finances. So she had to empathize with Wyatt's own troubles where his uncle was concerned.

"What about Gladdy?" Wyatt asked finally. "She doesn't think she's in love with Leo, does she?"

"I have no idea. I couldn't believe they were holding hands under the table. It's like something twelve-year-olds would do."

Jane felt awful remembering that soft, warm glow on Gladdy's face. She'd looked delighted with their intimate dinner at first, and Jane had simply thought Gladdy was happy for Gram, silly as that would be, because Gladdy didn't believe in love any more than Gram did.

"They've never fought over a man before," Jane confided. "And they grew up together, moved into their first apartment together and have lived together off and on ever since. The thought of a man coming between them is unthinkable."

And yet, Jane had seen with her very own eyes the way Gladdy looked at Leo and Leo looked at her. And Gram!

That little weasel of an eighty-six-year-old man!

"I suppose we could start by talking to Gladdy," Wyatt offered. "Appeal to her sense of friendship and devotion to your grandmother, and at the same time, tell her the sad, hard truth about Leo. That might, at least, keep him from coming between the two women."

Jane nodded sadly. "It would be a start."

"Just tell me what you want, Jane. I'll do whatever you think would be best. If you want me to talk to Gladdy, I will. I'll be unmerciful in explaining Leo's lifelong habits with women."

"Short of hog-tying your uncle to his bed and locking him in his room—"

"Believe me, I've wished I could."

Which actually had Jane smiling a bit.

Wyatt Gray was a reasonable man, and Jane had found that so few men were. She regretted how things had started out between them.

"I'm sorry if I behaved badly toward you at first," she said, because a polite, well-bred, empowered woman always acknowledged her own unfair treatment of others and apologized. "Gram and Gladdy... Well, I just adore them both, and looking out for them hasn't always been easy, but believe me, they need someone to look out for them and I try my best."

Wyatt gave her a reassuring smile and let one of his hands settle softly over hers on the table between them. "I'm sure you do your absolute best for everyone you care about."

Which was just so nice of him.

People sometimes thought Jane could be overzealous and maybe even a bit aggressive in her attempts to take care of others, when she truly never wanted to do anything but help. Women could just be so mixed up about some things, have such wrong ideas, and she felt it was her calling to straighten them out, to educate them, to help extricate them from the troubles they found themselves in. It wasn't a job to Jane. It was her calling, her mission in life.

"That's incredibly kind and generous of you," she admitted. "Especially when I yelled at you at first."

"It's completely forgotten," he promised, smiling once again.

She could see a bit of Leo in him when he smiled like that. The dangerous charm, that wicked twinkle in his eye. Not that he was flirting with her or anything like that. He'd been perfectly respectful during their exchange. Some men thought flirting was as natural and expected as breathing in any exchange between the sexes, even the most businesslike. Something of which Jane naturally disapproved.

But Wyatt hadn't been like that at all.

Still, the dangerous charm was there lurking below the surface in the man, even if he didn't turn it on every time with all women. But when he did...

Jane shivered just a bit, thinking he really was too good-looking for any woman's good and likely too used to getting his way with women, just as Leo was. She couldn't let herself forget that.

Not that Jane ever really forgot herself with a man.

"Well," she said, feeling a little warm and uneasy suddenly. "I suppose the best thing would be to talk to Gladdy first. I'll try it myself and see how it goes."

"And if that isn't enough, I'll talk to her. Just give me a call," Wyatt offered, pulling out a business card and scribbling down a phone number on it. "My office and personal numbers. Feel free to call anytime, Jane."

She pulled out a card of her own, wrote her private number on it and handed it over to him. Picking up his card, she saw Wyatt Addison Gray IV, attorney at law, with what she knew was a pricey downtown address.

"What kind of law?" she asked.

"Divorce." His mouth twitched, trying to hold back what she suspected would be a mind-numbingly gorgeous grin. "I have to admit, it seemed to come naturally to me. I saw so many of them in my family as I was growing up."

Jane nodded. "Me too. What was the longest marriage in your family?"

"Leo's last one. Eleven years."

"Wow. Impressive," Jane declared. "We never managed to do better than six."

Wyatt shrugged, as if to say, *What are you going to do?*

"I think we're going to work together well to handle this little problem," Jane told him, quite pleased with herself and Mr. Wyatt Addison Gray, Esquire.

"I do, too, Jane."

Jane felt like a dynamo the next morning, charging through her routine with even more enthusiasm and effectiveness than usual. Powering through her morning kickboxing class, getting to the office early, proofing the copy for her latest ad campaign for her Fabulous Female Financial Boot Camp, even sketching out ideas for a series of advanced classes for women who'd mastered the principles laid out in the first seminar.

She felt like she could do anything.

Her assistant, Lainie, showed up at the usual time, looking puzzled at the way Jane rattled off a list of things she already needed Lainie to take care of.

"You didn't have one of those energy drinks again, did you?" Lainie asked. "I told you, Jane, your system really can't handle those. You're already on overdrive. You don't need the boost."

"Of course not." Jane looked puzzled. "After all, a well-rested, well-nourished woman doesn't need artificial stimulants."

She reached for her notepad, always close at hand, and started scribbling.

"Sorry," she said, quite pleased with herself. "I need to write that down. I'm thinking about working on a book of my philosophies. Financial advice for women is such a nice niche market these days, and it would be a wonderful cross-promotion for my seminars. Don't you think?"

"Sure," Lainie said, still frowning.

"What?"

"It's just that…you seem…happy."

"I am almost always happy," Jane insisted.

Lainie looked skeptical. "I think you might have been whistling when I walked in."

Jane thought back. Had she been? And what if she was?

"How did things go with your grandmother yesterday? Did you meet this man she claims to love?"

"Oh, yes," Jane said. "A complete cad, but Wyatt and I will take care of the situation."

"Wyatt?"

"The man's nephew. Wyatt Addison Gray IV. I have to say, I disliked him on sight as we sat down to dinner, but then we went across the street to this bar and had drinks afterward, and he was completely open and honest and reasonable. Altogether, a remarkable man."

Lainie gaped at her. "You met a man you think is reasonable?"

Jane nodded.

"And honest?"

"I told you, a remarkable man," Jane repeated even more emphatically than before.

"And you had dinner and drinks? Like…a date?"

"I date," Jane insisted.

"Not in this calendar year," Lainie reminded her.

"I'm just very selective about the men I find worthy of my consideration and time."

Lainie's bottom lip curled over her teeth, and she looked like she might bite herself to keep from replying to that, but finally gave up the battle and said, "And when you do, you don't show up in the office whistling the next morning. If I didn't know you better, I'd say you and Wyatt Gray didn't end things with dinner and drinks last night."

"Of course we did. I would never take a man home with me that I'd just met, and going home with him would be just as risky and irresponsible." And Jane never took irresponsible risks. "Besides, this wasn't a date. It was dinner at the retirement park with Gram, Gladdy and Wyatt's uncle, the cad. Assessing the situation we're facing with them."

"And the drinks afterward?" Lainie prompted.

"A place to talk without them present, where Wyatt and I found out that we're in complete agreement that the relationship between his uncle and Gram has to be stopped. We plotted our strategy to make that happen."

"Of course," Lainie said. "I just got so excited when you said you met a man you think is reasonable."

"Well, I'm sure there are a few of them in the world," Jane admitted.

Granted, that might be considered a rather large concession on her part to the quality of men alive on the planet at this moment. But she did consider herself a reasonable woman, and a reasonable woman would have to concede that Wyatt Gray had not been what she'd first thought.

"I'll even admit we had a very interesting and enlightening conversation," Jane said, thinking she was being exceedingly reasonable and fair-minded now.

"Okay, tell the truth. He's gorgeous, isn't he?" Lainie asked with a knowing gleam in her eyes.

"That had absolutely nothing to do with...anything," Jane insisted, thinking, oddly, that she felt a little...tingly inside and just a tad overly warm all of a sudden.

How odd.

Lainie laughed.

"It didn't," Jane corrected. "You know I always say the worst thing in the world a woman can do, besides depend on a man financially, is to judge one by his looks. I would never, ever do that. In fact, the best-looking men are almost always the most spoiled and immature."

It was true. She knew it. Long experience with the women in her family had proven it.

"We must be talking Greek God in a designer suit here," Lainie claimed.

"He was beautifully dressed," Jane admitted, again only trying to be fair.

And still, feeling that unusual, unsettling tingly warmth inside her.

"You know, I may be coming down with something," she told Lainie. "Does it feel warm in here to you? Could you check to see if anyone messed with the thermostat?"

Chapter Four

Jane waited until Gram was at her regular tennis lesson two days later, because normally Gram and Gladdy were practically inseparable, and then went to do her duty, to save poor Gladdy from Wyatt's ill-behaved uncle.

Jane pasted on a fake smile, walked into Gladdy's room, and—

"Oh, my God!"

It looked like Gladdy and Leo were…necking on the love seat! Gladdy had her head on Leo's shoulder, and his was bent over hers. When Jane burst in, Gladdy gave a start and her head popped up, banging into Leo's forehead.

Jane stood there, astonished and really, really mad on both Gladdy's and Gram's behalf.

"Oh, Jane, dear, will you ever learn to knock?" Gladdy asked, practically giggling.

Giggling?

Jane worked herself up into a good, steaming rage and pointed her finger at Leo, who didn't look guilty in the least over what he'd done. "You," she said, advancing on him. "Get your hands off my aunt! Right now! Now!"

She'd beat him off with her briefcase if she had to. Jane lifted it up and back, preparing to take a swing.

Leo Gray stood up, all too slowly for Jane's current mood, smoothed out his shirt, brushed back the bit of hair on the sides of his head and looked for all the world like he was the insulted party here.

"Girly," he said. "You've got to learn to have a little fun."

Jane's mouth fell open.

Girly?

He'd called her *Girly!*

"I'll have you know that I am a twenty-eight-year-old adult woman! I am no girl," she yelled after him, as he left Gladdy's room. "I should have you arrested for this!"

"Arrested?" Gladdy said, taking her arm and pulling the briefcase out of her hand. "Jane, what are you doing?"

"I came to warn you about that awful man! Did he force himself on you? Tell me, because if he did, I'll—"

"Leo Gray's never had to force himself on a woman in his life," Gladdy insisted. "I mean, have you looked at the man? I know you're not seventy-five years old like me—"

"Gladdy, you're eighty," Jane reminded her.

"Shhhh. He doesn't know that. A woman should never admit to her real age and never look her real age. There's no reason to in these days. Speaking of which, Jane, darling, is it too much to ask for you to use that nice age-resistant face cream Kathleen and I bought you for Christmas? You have beautiful skin, dear, but you want to keep it that way. You'll care about these things one day. At least, I pray that you will."

"That I'll worry about wrinkles one day? That's what you pray for?"

"No, that you'll learn how to enjoy a man and want to look your best for him."

Jane sank down into the love seat Leo had just vacated, suddenly so tired and frustrated, she could have cried or screamed. That awful man!

"Are you sure you're all right?" she asked Gladdy.

"Of course, I'm all right. I'm better than I've been in years, in fact. Nothing like a fabulous man to make a woman feel young again. I think I'm going to get my hair done and have a facial. What do you say, Jane? A facial? My treat?"

Jane felt like she might turn into a stark raving lunatic at any moment. "A facial? Gladdy?"

"Good skin care is nothing to scoff at, Jane."

"What about Gram? You love Gram. You always have, and she thinks she's in love with that man, that awful man—"

"He's far from awful, and Kathleen has never been in love in her life," Gladdy insisted. "You know that. You know what the women in our family are like."

"Yes, but she told me that she loves him. I've never heard her sound this way, and if she knew what the two of you were doing behind her back… Not even behind her back," Jane remembered. "The other night, at dinner?"

"We were holding hands. It's hardly a crime, hardly anything at all. What a prude you can be sometimes, Jane. I just hate that for you. I want you to be happy in every way, including having a man in your life."

"Prude?" Jane was so hurt, she could hardly speak.

Frustrated, infuriating tears filled her eyes. *Prude?* "I am not!"

"You're objecting to hand-holding, my darling. If that isn't prudish, I don't know what is. I was holding hands with boys in first grade."

Jane gasped, hurt. *Prude?* She opened her mouth to object again, and then realized if she didn't get out of there right that minute, she was going to cry. And Jane Carlton never cried, especially in front of anyone!

"I…I…I have to go. I can't talk to you about this right now," she said, then got up and fled.

She was outside, hurrying down the walkway toward her car, not really watching as carefully as she should have been, when she literally ran right into Leo Gray.

"You," she said, "Necking with my aunt? Behind my grandmother's back! My grandmother who thinks she's in love with you? You rat!"

He didn't crumple or anything from the impact of their collision. The man was solid for his age. But then he grabbed her by the arms. She hated grabby men.

"Get your hands off me this instant!" she yelled.

"Calm down, girly," he said, having the nerve to seem amused. "I'm just trying to make sure you don't fall down."

"I don't need any help to keep from falling down. Let go of me this instant!"

She jerked herself away with everything she had, but he was stronger than he looked, and he didn't let go. A haze of red came over Jane's vision. She was so mad now, she couldn't even see, couldn't remember ever being this mad in her life.

It was all his fault!

Every bit of it!

Her grandmother would be brokenhearted. He'd been necking with Gladdy, Gladdy who'd called Jane a prude! And this awful man had the nerve to tell her she needed to relax?

Before she truly thought of what she was about to do, Jane pulled back the hand with her briefcase and got ready to whack him with it. She got the backswing in and was bringing her hand forward when, only then, her mind cleared just a bit so she could actually see what she was doing.

She was about to hit an old man.

A nearly ninety-year-old man!

"Oh, my God!" she cried, changing her mind right at the end of her backswing, as she started swinging her arm forward.

Could she stop it now? Was it too late?

And then she gasped as she was lifted off her feet—literally—and hauled around in the other direction.

Wyatt saw Jane and Leo having what looked like angry words, but he wasn't really worried at first.

Then Leo put his hands on Jane, holding on to her.

Not the smartest thing to do, Wyatt was sure.

Then he saw Jane wind up to take a swing at Leo with her briefcase.

"Good God! Jane!" he yelled, barely getting to her in time.

He was in the wrong place to get between her and Leo. He was behind Jane. So he just put an arm around her waist, hauled her back against him and swung her around the other way.

Leo ducked and her briefcase went flying, landing harmlessly in the petunias in the flower bed to the right.

She screamed in pure outrage, like she was being mugged in a dark alley, kicking her feet in the air, her arms coming back to grab him. She hit him in the eye, then grabbed and thankfully got nothing but his hair. Afterward she took that handful of hair and yanked hard.

"Jane," he hollered at first, because she wouldn't have heard him over the racket she was making otherwise. "It's Wyatt. Shhhh. I'm not going to hurt you. I would never hurt you."

He got another arm around her, this one across her hips, her body completely plastered against his as he spoke softly into her right ear. "Shhh. It's all right."

She stopped kicking out with her feet, stopped squirming and went still. Maybe that was even worse, because then her hips were pressed against his abdomen—sweet, curvy Jane hips. She was breathing hard, and as he lowered her to her feet, her whole body rubbed along his.

Damn, Jane.

She really would be outraged if she knew the direction of his thoughts at the moment.

He put her down and she turned around, right there in front of him, looking shocked, still more than a little mad, and all rumpled and…sexy.

Very, very sexy.

Her hair had come tumbling down from that well-disciplined knot she'd had it in yesterday. It tumbled about her shoulders and her face. Her cheeks were flushed, eyes glistening with unshed tears.

A look of horror came over her face as she glanced from him to Leo to the crowd of retirees Wyatt now realized had come to watch this scene.

"Oh, my God!" she said, like she'd just woken up from a nightmare.

He took her carefully by the arms, to steady her and nothing more, not because he just needed to have his hands on her. "It's okay," he promised quietly, then turned and addressed the crowd. "Everybody's fine here. Just a slight misunderstanding. Let's all move along now. Nothing to see."

Jane's mouth fell open, and for a moment, it looked like she was going to hide her face against Wyatt's chest to keep from having to see anyone. Not that he had any objections.

He had the feeling Jane Carlton very seldom, if ever, let herself really lose it like that, and while he wasn't a man to condone violence, he had to admit, if any man could push a woman over the edge, it would be one of the Gray men. Leo probably deserved to be whacked with much more than the briefcase.

His mouth twitched. He was aching to grin, but tried to maintain his stern facade as Leo came cautiously closer. Wyatt eased Jane's face against him in a loose embrace, while she hid for a moment.

Over the top of her head, he mouthed to Leo, "What the hell did you do now?"

Leo shook his head, pretending an innocence Wyatt was sure was completely fake.

"Get out of here," he mouthed.

Before he turned Jane loose on the man.

Wyatt waited until Leo was far enough away. He felt fairly certain Jane wouldn't chase after him, if she saw him, and then reluctantly stepped away from her.

She was shaking and felt so tiny in his arms. "You okay now?" he asked.

When she finally lifted her head, she looked a bit dazed and still horrified. "I can't believe I did that."

Again, Wyatt had to fight not to grin, because she looked like she was confessing to mass murder.

"Leo's fine," he said. "Not a scratch on him."

"I almost hit another person!" she cried. "An old man!"

"Now that would offend him terribly. Calling him an old man and thinking he was too frail to take you on in a fight."

"I don't fight!" Jane cried. "I can't… I would never… I've always been devoted to nonviolent ways of settling disagreements. I abhor violence in any form."

"An admirable principle," Wyatt assured her.

"But I could have really hurt him. I mean, I take kick-boxing and self-defense classes."

Wyatt couldn't help it. He chuckled at that.

Jane, kickboxing? It was laughable, given her size. If her little suits weren't so severely cut, he'd swear she had to shop in the girl's department.

"I could have hurt him," she insisted. "I've had abused women go through my seminars. And every now and then, a man gets mad at the things I've taught a woman and shows up at the office. I thought it was important to learn to protect myself, that every woman should."

"Of course," Wyatt agreed. Mad men came looking for her? Pint-size Jane? He didn't like the sound of that at all.

"But I never believed I could resort to anything like that myself. Wyatt, this is horrible. This is completely unacceptable. One minute, I was fine, and the next, I just saw red, literally, and I was taking a swing at him."

"Jane, I've nearly decked him a time or two myself, and I assure you that I too abhor violence. I've had abused women in my office, as well, trying to work up the courage to divorce their abusers."

"I'm so sorry," she said, still aghast at her own behavior, standing on the walkway at the retirement park, looking around like she'd just found herself on another planet.

"It's all right. I promise. And I'm sorry I grabbed you like that. I was just trying to keep you from hitting him."

"And I'm so glad you did."

"What did he do to make you so mad?"

"I went to talk to Gladdy about him, and I caught them necking in her room! And he was so awful! He called me names and said I just needed to learn to have some fun. Fun! He's going to hurt my grandmother and Gladdy's feelings terribly, and he thinks it's fun!"

Jane realized she'd said it like *fun* was a dirty word, which she didn't believe, and she wasn't really a prude, was she?

"But I wasn't really going to hit him, Wyatt, I swear! I changed my mind. Midway through that swing, I realized what I was doing and changed my mind. I just wasn't sure if I could stop in time. My briefcase was already headed for him, and I just… I don't… This is sooo awful!"

"Jane, it's fine. Everyone's fine."

"And then you grabbed me, and I didn't know it was you, and I—"

"I know. I didn't mean to manhandle you. I just had to act fast, and…well, I'm sorry."

And then she looked horrified again, raised her hand to the side of his face and said, "I hit you!"

His right eye throbbed a bit. "It's nothing," he insisted.

"No. It's turning red and a little puffy." She touched it, with her fingertips, featherlight, trying to find the extent of the blow. "Oh, my God, Wyatt! I could have put your eye out!"

"I seriously doubt that."

"No, I've been trained to do that." She seemed absolutely convinced that she could. "A man attacks you, you go for the eyes. It's one of the most vulnerable spots on the body. Eyes, nose with the heel of your hand, groin—"

"Okay, thankfully, I came out of this unscathed."

"No, we have to get something on that eye. Ohhh," she fretted. "I feel awful about this. You have to let me help you."

"Well, if you insist," he said, turning himself over to her tender care.

Gladdy, Leo and Kathleen watched from the cover of the rhododendrons fifteen feet away.

"Ladies, I'm afraid I overplayed the scene," Leo said.

"Nonsense. Jane overreacted," Gram stated. "Gladdy and I should have warned you about that. Poor Jane does tend to overreact."

"She's got some fire in her, all right. I like that in a woman," Leo admitted. "Couldn't believe she actually took a swing at me. Didn't think she had it in her."

"It was the 'girly' remark," Gladdy said. "And I may have overplayed things a bit myself with her."

"Of course not. It worked perfectly," Kathleen insisted. "Look at them. Jane feels terrible about what she did and Wyatt's comforting her. It's so sweet. They've known each other for less than three days and there they are. I'd say our plan to get them together is a rousing success."

"Well, in that case, ladies," Leo said, "would you care to join me for a celebratory drink? I have champagne chilling in the minifridge in my room. We can decide on our next move and commemorate the success of this one."

* * *

Wyatt took Jane back to his apartment, which was a mere four blocks away—a sleek, shiny, modern, expensive loft in a high-rise on the edge of town.

Jane taking charge was something to behold. She pushed him down to sit in the middle of the big, cushy sofa the minute they had walked in the door, and told him not to move. He complied.

She got ice from the kitchen, lectured him mildly about the need to take care of himself properly once she found out he didn't even have an ice pack, explained that one should always be prepared for life's emergencies, then said they'd make do with a ziplock bag wrapped in a hand towel.

She came to stand behind him, took his head in her hands and eased it back against the sofa cushions. Then she placed the makeshift ice pack on his right eye.

"Keep that there while I search your bathroom. You must have some ointment and bandages somewhere."

He sprawled on the couch, leaning back as instructed and holding the ice to his eye. He never imagined a woman giving orders to him would be so sexy. Normally, he was a take-charge kind of guy. Not that he ordered women around, either. Just that…well, he couldn't help but wonder now exactly how Jane would be in bed.

Would all those spitfire tendencies come out? That take-charge attitude, demanding what she wanted from him?

Wyatt had a hard time imagining Jane knowing what she truly wanted in bed, much less demanding it. She was cute, but didn't seem to have much use for men, and any woman who'd been truly satisfied in bed would have at least one use for a man, he reasoned. He suspected she was very good at pushing men away, at keeping them at arm's length, and not that good at really letting herself go in any situation.

Not that he thought he'd see her in his bed anytime soon.

There had to be a dozen women he knew who'd be so much less trouble than Jane, although, he thought, once there, Jane would be interesting and definitely a challenge.

And Wyatt would admit to being a man who liked a challenge.

She came back a moment later and he felt the couch cushions give with her weight, as she knelt on the seat beside him, bracing her side on the back of the couch as she leaned over him.

Removing the ice pack, she frowned down at him, her face maybe an inch from his as she inspected his eye.

"It's all red and puffy now," she complained, sighing heavily, her warm breath brushing across his cheek, his ear.

He shivered just a bit, wondering what she'd do if he pushed her backward to lay on the couch, stretched out on top of her and started giving a few orders of his own. Would she give him a smile and wind her arms around him? More likely, she'd try to hit him again or really put his eye out this time.

The woman thought she was a champion kickboxer, after all.

Wyatt grinned, laughing a bit, unable to help himself.

"What? There's nothing funny about this. I feel terrible, Wyatt."

"Well, I don't," he said. "It's really nothing, Jane. I can hardly feel it anymore. I assure you, I'm fine." As long as she didn't figure out where his thoughts were going at the moment.

She put the ice pack aside and came up with some kind of ointment, which she then very carefully spread with her fingertips along his eyelid, his brow and the side of his face. And as she got closer and concentrated harder on getting it in exactly the right place and not his eye, her body leaned into the side of his, one breast pressed against his shoulder.

He felt like someone had installed a giant neon Trouble sign in his apartment when he wasn't looking, and that it had just flickered on and was blinking in a fire-engine red color.

Trouble, trouble, trouble!

He had real problems to deal with. Leo and his penchant for getting kicked out of retirement complexes had Wyatt worried that there would be no place in all of Maryland that would take his uncle, once Ms. Steele put the word out about him. And the easiest way to fix that problem was for Wyatt and Jane to work together.

If he made her mad, came on to her, offended her, hurt her, he doubted they'd be working together to solve the Leo problem any longer. So Ms. Jane Carlton was definitely off-limits. It would be more trouble in the long run than any short-term fling with her would be worth.

So what if she smelled really good? And had the sweetest, gentlest touch in a little spitfire of a body? Which he suspected no man had ever properly awakened before. Surely he was capable of exercising some kind of discipline where a woman was concerned.

He shifted his weight, thinking to ease away from her, and instead, set her off balance and her whole body fell against his. No question now. Those were her breasts pressed against him, her neck and her sweet, sassy Jane mouth right at the corner of his own.

She gasped in surprise, her eyes suddenly all big and round and so close to his, not blinking. Neither of them breathed for an instant.

He could have her flat on her back in a moment. Or take her by her thighs and pull her across his lap facing him, palm those pretty hips he'd had pressed against him earlier and pull her tight against him. He knew it, and if he knew anything about women, she was thinking the same thing.

Discipline, Wyatt. It's not just a word.

"Jane," he whispered, hardly able to believe he was actually doing this, taking her arms in his hands and steadying her, then easing her away from him, to sit on her knees on the cushion beside him. "I'm sorry. I didn't mean to throw you off balance like that."

She just looked at him, sexy and baffled and maybe embarrassed, which was the last thing he wanted.

"And I'm just not sure what you want here," he confessed. "But I know what I want, and I really don't want to offend you."

She seemed a little dazed, innocent. *Damn.*

"What I want?"

"Yes," he said.

"I…I was just trying to fix your eye."

"Okay." He smiled what he hoped was an I-understand-perfectly smile and not an I-wanted-to-jump-your-bones one. "That's what I thought you were doing. My mistake."

"Mistake?"

She looked a little sad then, a little embarrassed. He could feel her withdrawing from him, even though she hadn't actually moved an inch.

"I'm just… I'm a guy, okay? Some women would say, I'm not a very nice guy. That I…well, when a woman gets this close and is…touching me…I get ideas. Ideas that, I'm afraid, were not the same ideas you were having, and… well, you're a beautiful woman, Jane."

She scrambled to get off the couch, to get away from him, hot color blooming in her cheeks as she got all flustered. "You thought…I was coming on to you?"

He nodded, thinking honesty probably wasn't the best policy here, that he'd offended her, when, he swore to God, he'd been trying to do the exact opposite. To keep from offending her.

Women. They could just be so hard to read, and sometimes it seemed there was no way to win. No way at all.

Come on to her and offend her? Don't come on to her and still offend her?

What was a guy to do?

"I am so sorry," she said.

"Jane, it's no big deal—

She blushed even more furiously. "I would never—"

"Never?" Now that hurt. "Never?"

"I'm not… I mean to say, I don't—"

"Don't what?" Now he had to know. Never with anyone? No way. Not in this day and age. Or no way, no how, with him? That seemed like overstating it a bit. "What do you mean, never?"

"I don't…throw myself at men."

Okay, that he believed, though in his thoroughly male opinion it was a shame.

The world should be full of women who threw themselves at men. Of course, it was, he'd found, but not many of those women were like Jane.

"I'm sorry. For everything. And I just… I have to go," she said.

"You really don't," he claimed.

"I do." She turned and fled.

Wyatt swore softly and succinctly, his body humming with desire, still feeling her pressed against him, her soft hands on his face.

He was an idiot. A complete idiot where women like her were concerned.

Chapter Five

Jane Carlton did not come on to men.

At least, she didn't think she did.

She didn't mean to.

Her face burned when she remembered being on the couch with Wyatt the day before. He'd thought she was making a pass at him? And he'd been trying to say…he'd welcome that?

Surely not.

"You're frowning again," Lainie said, standing in the doorway with a batch of message slips with Jane's calls on them. "What in the world happened to you yesterday?"

Jane, if puzzling over anyone's behavior except Wyatt's, would have normally turned to Gram and Gladdy for advice on men. Between the two of them, she doubted there was any situation Jane might find herself in that they hadn't already been in themselves. But she couldn't talk to them about Wyatt. Not when she was trying to keep his uncle away from both of them.

She figured Lainie was her best shot for help here.

"Can I ask you something about men?" Jane blurted out before she lost her nerve.

Lainie giggled.

"Why is that so funny?" Jane asked, finding Lainie's reaction slightly offensive, maybe more than slightly.

"It's not funny. I'm just so happy, Jane!" she said, like Jane had announced she was eloping or something.

"It's just a question."

"Okay. Go ahead. Please." Lainie sounded so eager. "Anything I can do to help."

"You think I need help with men?"

"Oh, definitely."

No hesitation there. Jane pictured herself as a virtual wrecking yard of relationships, like there might be a sign that said, *Abandon all hope, ye who enter here.*

"It's about…coming on to men," she said, wishing she'd never started this whole thing.

"Oh!" Lainie clapped her hands together like a kid who'd just received a terrific present. "This is sooooo good! Jane, I'm so proud of you. You actually want to make the first move with a man!"

"No, I didn't say that. I'm just…trying to find out if I already did."

"Well, that's even better! Tell me! Tell me everything," she begged.

Jane thought about how she might explain, then decided it would probably be better to just show Lainie. There was a love seat in Jane's office, after all.

"Shut the door," she instructed, then got up and walked

over to the love seat. "I just…sit down and let me show you."

"Okay." Lainie sat.

Jane knelt on the love seat, conscious now of how hard it was to keep her balance. "Lean your head back."

Lainie did, and Jane eased closer.

"Now, you've hurt your eye, and I'm…I'm trying to fix it. That's it. Just trying to fix it. Like this, except you're a lot taller than me, so I had to reach up higher. If I did that, would you think I was coming on to you?"

She reached up to a point past Lainie's eye and then looked down and realized her breasts were practically in Lainie's face when she made that move.

"Oh, no!" Jane cried.

Lainie lifted her head before Jane could move away, and then…sure enough, breasts in her face.

While Lainie giggled, Jane went to brace herself against Lainie's body to get out of the way, but before she could do that, she heard a voice.

A man's voice, Wyatt's, clearing his throat and then saying, "Ladies, I'm so sorry. There was no one at the desk out front, and I…seem to have caught you at a bad time."

Jane froze, her mouth dropping open.

This could not be happening.

Lainie looked over Jane's shoulder. She could see Lainie taking the whole thing in. Mulling it over. Wyatt, how gorgeous he was. His eye, no doubt at least a bit bruised. Jane's worry about coming on to a man. Jane shoving her breasts practically in his face while she tried to fix his eye and needing to reenact the whole scene to figure that out.

She was a complete idiot.

She looked to Lainie, mouthing, *Don't leave me. Please don't leave me alone with him. Please!*

"Sorry." Lainie laughed and got up from the couch. "I'm sure I have…something to do at my desk."

Jane hung her head down and stayed there, sat back on her heels on the love seat, thinking if she never had to turn around and look at him, she might live through this day with just a shred of her dignity intact.

She heard Lainie introduce herself and Wyatt's gloriously deep, beautiful voice saying, "Wyatt Gray. So nice to meet you."

And then Lainie disappeared, closing the door behind her.

Jane stayed where she was and said, "If I paid you…like a million dollars, would you turn around and go away? So that we never had to talk about this?"

He laughed. Beautifully. The sound like a current zinging through her body.

And then he walked over and sat down beside her. She still perched there on her knees, not wanting to shove any part of herself into his face, either accidentally or on purpose.

He looked like a man who couldn't be more pleased with himself or his life at this moment. Wearing a gorgeously expensive suit that wrapped faithfully around his altogether impressive body, he sat there, slightly blackened eye and all, looking completely at ease and holding a huge bouquet of exotic-looking flowers in his hand.

"Jane, I'm seldom wrong about these things, but with you… Well, I suppose it's a possibility. I just haven't had a lot of dealings with women like you. You don't…like women, do you?"

"What? Of course, I like women. Women are great, women are—"

"Sexually," he clarified.

"Oh. You mean…me and Lainie? Me and…women? That way?"

He nodded.

"No! I… No! Not that there's anything wrong with that. But, I like men." She got all flustered then, and kept talking, which she tended to do when flustered. Fill the silence and try to move on. "Granted, not a lot of men. But I do…like…men. I mean, I have to admit I like them more in theory than reality, but… Well… Oh, my God!"

She buried her head in her hands and gave up.

Too much information, Jane.

Way too much information.

"Well, I'm happy to hear that," Wyatt responded. "That you like men. And that you find at least a few of us…acceptable and interesting."

The flowers, looking lush, exotic and expensive, came into her field of view, even with her head hanging low so she didn't have to look at him.

"These are for you," he continued, still sounding amused. "A small token of apology, nothing else. No reason for you to worry."

"But *I* hit *you*," she said, taking the flowers and feeling completely inadequate at the moment as a girl. This whole girl-stuff thing had just never come naturally to her. Or maybe she just hadn't tried hard enough or cared enough. But she'd always felt a little awkward in this area.

Even more than usual with Wyatt.

"I know, but I embarrassed you yesterday in my apartment, and it certainly wasn't my intention."

"No. It was me. I was… I'm so sorry—"

"Jane," he interrupted. "Take the flowers and say thank you. Then forget about the whole thing. It's as easy as that."

Easy for him, maybe.

"Jane?" He touched his fingers gently to her chin and urged her to raise her head and look him in the eye.

His poor, bruised eye. It was a faded black shade. She'd really hit a man.

"I'm telling everyone a hulking two-hundred-fifty-pound man did this to me, and that I got it defending a lady's honor. My female clients are impressed and the men are intimidated."

She was sure the women were impressed.

"Take the flowers and say 'thank you,'" he reminded her.

She took them and mumbled, "Thank you."

He sat there looking as relaxed and gorgeous as could be, despite the black eye. "Now, what are we going to do about Leo and your sweet grandmother and great aunt?"

Two days later, Jane was in the middle of a youth-regenerating apricot-mint facial and pedicure—thinking it would give her some alone time with Gladdy to explain what a rat Leo really was—when she got the call.

Ms. Steele, the Remington Park administrator, insisted on seeing her immediately.

That had never happened before.

Jane promised to be there within the hour because Gladdy insisted that no meeting was worth cutting short a facial and pedicure.

As she sat in the waiting area outside Ms. Steele's office, Jane had a sinking feeling she knew what this was about. That Ms. Steele had heard about Jane attempting to slug Leo Gray on the grounds of Remington Park.

How humiliating!

She remembered it seemed like tons of eyes were staring at her when that freakish red haze cleared—when she stopped trying to kick Wyatt in the shins and pull out his hair, thinking she was under attack and all her self-defense training she'd never had to use before was kicking in. So it wasn't that surprising Ms. Steele would have heard about it. From what Jane had seen in the time Gram and Gladdy had been here, Ms. Steele kept a very close eye on the goings-on at Remington Park. As a business owner, Jane could only applaud that kind of devotion and attention to detail.

But at the moment, she was horribly embarrassed.

She sat there getting more and more nervous, wondering how in the world she might explain herself, when Wyatt, blackened eye and all, strolled in.

Her face fell. "You've been summoned, too?"

He nodded, taking the seat beside her, looking much more at ease here than she did.

"I feel like I've been called into the principal's office," Jane fretted.

He laughed. "I'm going out on a limb here, but I bet you were a very good girl growing up, Jane. I bet you've never been called to the principal's office before."

"Only for good things. Like accepting awards and organizing school fund-raisers," she admitted, sighing heavily. "How in the world am I going to explain getting into a fight on the grounds of my grandmother and aunt's retirement park?"

"Denial is always a good start," he began.

"Denial? You're sitting here with a black eye."

"And if denial is out of the question, I recommend, as a next step, downplaying the importance and scope of the situation."

"You sound like a defense attorney now. Either that or someone who's used to being in trouble."

He shook his head. "Never been a defense attorney, but I did play one in moot court competition in law school. Won my cases every time."

Jane wasn't surprised about the wins and noted he hadn't denied being in trouble himself. She shook her head and said, "I got Gladdy alone today at a salon. It was like talking to a Barbie doll. She ignored everything I said about your uncle and kept suggesting new skin care routines for me."

"Wait…salon?" He leaned in close, his nose practically touching the rim of her ear, sniffing her hair, then the side of her face. "Is that why you smell so good? Good enough to eat?"

She closed her eyes, feeling all tingly and warm at the same time.

Because a man was sniffing her youth-regenerating apricot-mint facial?

She felt him breathing in that smell, the heat from his body so close, radiating toward hers. The tip of his nose gently brushed her cheek. Was it an accident?

"What is it? Peaches?"

"Apricots," she admitted, not daring to move an inch.

She didn't think she'd ever had actual sexual intercourse that felt this good. Her breasts ached and she thought she wanted to shove them into his face right now. She could spread apricot-mint facial cream over her whole body and then practice her coming-on-to-him skills and see how he liked it.

Jane was even regretting wearing her customary white, no-frills, all-buttoned-up blouse, because honestly, how much good could a woman do trying to stick her breasts in a man's face when she was buttoned up practically to her chin? She was even considering undoing a few buttons, as unobtrusively as possible, when she heard a door open.

There was dead silence for a moment.

A throat was cleared quite pointedly.

When Jane glanced up, Ms. Steele, looking particularly steelish at the moment, was gaping at them both.

Face flaming, Jane turned to Wyatt. Sitting up straight in his chair now, he threw up his hands in a helpless manner and mouthed, "Sorry," before standing, extending a hand to Jane, then leading her into Ms. Steele's office.

They sat side by side in front of Ms. Steele's desk. Jane looked determinedly down at the floor so she couldn't see Wyatt, but she felt him, absolutely certain he was doing that easy yet elegant sprawl of his, perfectly comfortable in that chair, ready to brazen this out with the body language that said, *Problem? There is no problem here.*

The man had nerve, and it seemed he was impossible to embarrass.

What in the world must Ms. Steele think of them?

"I am so sorry for that…that…" What to call it? Jane couldn't think of a thing and sat there mute, feeling stupid all over again.

Wyatt shot her a hard look that said something like… *Denial and downplaying, remember? You're not helping, Jane.*

Jane dared to look up at Ms. Steele, who appeared to

be having a hard time believing what she'd just seen in her waiting room.

"I…" the woman began. "I wasn't aware that the two of you knew each other."

"Oh, we don't," Jane claimed, then realized how ridiculous that sounded, given the fact that they were just in the waiting room, Wyatt practically nuzzling her cheek. Would what he did really be considered nuzzling? Or had he just been smelling her fruity facial? "My grandmother, my aunt and Wyatt's uncle introduced us. They know each other. That's all."

"Oh, I'm aware that they know each other," she said, emphasis on the word *know.*

Jane felt like sinking down in her chair and trying to hide.

Wyatt, still brazening it out, asked, "Is there something we can do for you, Ms. Steele?"

The woman's lips got all funny and stiff, as if she sternly disapproved of Wyatt, maybe of both of them. Jane couldn't be sure.

"You could tell me," Ms. Steele said, "why I have very odd and difficult-to-believe, yet remarkably consistent reports, that you, Jane, attacked this man's uncle on the walkway outside the blue cottage shortly before noon yesterday."

Before she could say anything, Wyatt chuckled and said, "Oh, no. Nothing like that. She…uh…tripped. Jane wasn't looking where she was going. You know Jane, always on the move, always rushing about to get everything she has to get done…done. And she wasn't watching where she was going, and she tripped."

Now that was so brazen Jane couldn't help but admire his skill a bit. She supposed all lawyers lied. There were probably courses at law school on how to do it effectively. Wyatt Gray, no doubt, had excelled in those.

"I do know Jane," Ms. Steele said. "But I thought you two didn't know each other."

"Oh, just…you know…we were introduced one time by our relatives," Wyatt claimed. "And in fact, we all shared a very nice dinner at the blue cottage the other night. I have to say, the young woman working there, Amy I believe it was, makes outstanding lasagna. Doesn't she, Jane?"

Jane nodded. She'd be happy to talk about Amy and lasagna.

"So, Jane tripped, but she didn't get anywhere near my uncle, because I caught her," Wyatt said, not technically a lie. He had caught her. He pointed to his black eye and said, "That's how I got this."

Then he smiled that I-can-charm-any-woman-alive smile Jane had come to know so well. Except, sadly, Ms. Steele looked completely immune to it.

How could that be? Jane puzzled. She would have guessed no woman was truly immune to Wyatt at his gorgeous, most-charming self.

Ms. Steele cocked her head to the right and frowned at Wyatt. "So your story is… Jane tripped and you caught her?"

Wyatt nodded.

"You're nearly a foot taller than she is. How did you get hit in the eye?"

"I don't really know," Wyatt said. "It all happened so fast."

Ms. Steele rolled her eyes and gave a little huff, then turned to Jane. "I called you in here because I can't just ignore reports of fighting on the grounds of Remington Park. But I was sure it was Leo Gray who was responsible for this whole mess. I would never believe Jane attacked an old man for no reason."

"Oh, but…" *I did.*

Jane barely managed to stop herself as Wyatt clamped a hand down on hers. She took a breath, trying to think up some brazen lies of her own she might tell, but honestly, when was hitting an old man ever justified?

"It wasn't his fault. He didn't do anything to me. And I've never hit an old man in my life. I've never hit anyone…."

Except Wyatt.

He gave her a nod that said, *Well done, Jane.*

"I have no trouble believing the last part," Ms. Steele agreed, yet still seemed troubled.

"I am so sorry about this whole mix-up." Jane tried sounding her most earnest. "I strive to never cause trouble for anyone, and I'm sure Wyatt does, too. I've apologized profusely for giving him a black eye—"

"And I, of course, have forgiven her completely," he jumped in. "Knowing that it was most definitely unintentional on her part. So there's really no problem here."

With that, he got to his feet and urged Jane to do the same, as if his pronouncement that there was no problem was all that was needed to clear up this whole thing.

Jane smiled hopefully in Ms. Steele's direction, then did as Wyatt wanted and walked out the door ahead of him.

As he followed her, she could hear Ms. Steele call out to him, "We're not done with this, Mr. Gray."

Chapter Six

Wyatt thought they both deserved a drink after that little scene in Ms. Steele's office, and Jane, looking like she was still figuring out how her no-doubt neat, orderly life had come to this, let him steer her quite easily to the dark, quiet bar across the street. He set a drink in front of her before she ever uttered the first word of protest, and then she just sat there, looking bewildered, embarrassed and a little sad.

He really didn't want to make Jane sad.

"Why was Ms. Steele so sure this was all your uncle's fault?" she finally asked.

Wyatt frowned, wondering if he could bring himself to do the old denial-and-downplay routine with her.

No, he couldn't.

"Leo tends to…shake things up wherever he goes," he began, then had to admit that was definitely downplaying. "Actually, Jane, he chases after women like a man who's been celibate for years—which I'm sure he'd tell you feels like a reasonable equivalent of being married and faithful to one woman for the previous eleven years. And now that aunt Millicent is gone, he seems to feel the need to make up for lost time. He doesn't just go after one woman at a time. This thing with your grandmother and your aunt— I'm afraid it's not unusual at all for him. This is the norm."

She shook her head, disbelieving. "He's eighty-six!"

"I know. I keep hoping he'll get too tired for all of this, but so far…he hasn't even slowed down. He's been kicked out of three retirement homes, bringing complete chaos to the places. Women who've lived together happily for years suddenly turn on each other, when he favors one over the other, no matter how brief his attention span."

"He can't live by himself?" she suggested.

"He probably could, but he won't. You know how favorable the ratio of men to women is in these places. He thinks a retirement park is a paradise for men. And nothing I've said to him has been able to change him in any way. If he gets kicked out of Remington Park, I don't know what I'll do with him," Wyatt admitted. "And I'm truly sorry for any problems he might cause between your aunt and your grandmother."

"I love them so much," Jane said. "They make me crazy, but I just adore them."

"Yeah, I feel the same way about Leo. He was more of a father to me than my real father was. I mean, my father's not a bad guy or anything like that. He's just…well, he was more interested in his own life than mine. But Leo always took the time to look out for me, guide me, explain things to me. He was there if I needed help. I'd do anything for him."

"There should be some kind of pill to make men faithful," Jane said.

"If there was, Leo wouldn't take it."

"Well, I still feel like I have to apologize to him," she repeated. "I did take a swing at him, after all."

"I'm not sure he deserves an apology—"

"No, I have to. What I did was wrong, and I always apologize when I'm wrong."

"Okay." Wyatt nodded. "If you insist."

"I do. Will you come with me? Sometime tomorrow?"

"Of course."

They went to Leo's cottage, but he wasn't there.

Jane was a little afraid where they might find him and what he might be doing, but she was determined not to lose her good manners around him, at least not anymore. She felt oddly like her life could be on the verge of spinning off into complete chaos at any moment. How could that possibly have happened?

She couldn't blame it entirely on the Gray men. Her own behavior had been erratic, at best, and Jane preached that men could not make women crazy. Women allowed themselves to be crazy over men, but men could not force that kind of irrational behavior upon anyone. No one could. A woman was responsible for her own behavior at all times. She had to own her own decisions, her actions, her words, and Jane's had been abominable.

She and Wyatt walked into Gram and Gladdy's cottage.

Amy was in the kitchen, stirring something on the stove and baking something that smelled luscious. Leo Gray stood beside her. They both turned as the front door opened and Jane thought Amy looked particularly uncomfortable at the moment.

Jane frowned, whispering to Wyatt urgently. "He wouldn't hit on someone Amy's age. Would he?"

"I don't think so," Wyatt said. "But she doesn't look happy to have him here. Or maybe it's us. Maybe she thinks she's going to witness another scuffle."

Oh, Lord! He was probably right. Amy, sweet, kind, quiet little Amy, whom Jane wanted to help become a chef, had surely heard about Jane freaking out and attacking Leo Gray. Amy was looking at Jane like Jane had grown three heads.

"I will never live this down," she muttered.

"Come on," Wyatt said, putting a supportive hand at the small of her back and steering her to the kitchen. "Chin up. Smile. Be confident, gracious, polite. All the things I know you are, Jane. Put this behind you and move on."

"No. They all know." It wasn't her imagination. There were three little old ladies in the common area of the cottage, all staring at Jane like they'd never seen her before. "I'm infamous at Remington Park as the crazy woman who attacks old men with her briefcase!"

"Nonsense. One little slip does not a crazy woman make," Wyatt insisted.

They got to Leo and Amy's side, Amy now looking like she really wanted to run away, Leo looking calm and happy as could be, not at all like a man who created chaos everywhere he went.

"Hello, Amy," Wyatt said, turning on the charm. "I was just bragging to Ms. Steele yesterday about what an outstanding cook you are."

Amy blushed and stammered. "Uh…thank you. I'm making raspberry lemon bars."

"My favorite," Leo said, beaming.

Wyatt ignored that and did his best to charm and reassure Amy. "I'm sure they're lovely. I'm still thinking about the lasagna you made last week."

"I'll save you some to take home, if you're still here when they're done."

"Thank you, Amy. Now, could you excuse us a moment? Jane and I need to talk to my uncle."

"Of course," she said, looking uneasy again.

Wyatt gave a curt nod to Leo, to follow them into the empty dining area. He pulled out a chair for Jane, touching her reassuringly on her shoulder, then seated himself.

"She's not armed, is she?" Leo asked, still standing.

Jane felt like a worm, like one of the lowest creatures on earth and wished she could just crawl away right now.

"Uncle Leo?" Wyatt said none too softly.

Out of the corner of her eye, Jane saw Amy startle, heard the pan clatter on the stove like she'd lost control of it for a moment.

She was expecting the worst.

"Just sayin', you feeling better, girly?" Leo inquired.

"Now you're just trying to be annoying," Wyatt complained. "Let the lady explain why she's here."

"Mr. Gray," Jane began. "I am so very sorry about everything I did the other day, and I've come to humbly beg for your forgiveness. My behavior was completely unacceptable, and I am both shocked and humiliated that I resorted to violence as a way of settling our disagreement."

Leo grimaced, then shook his head. "Kathleen and Gladdy said you were kind of prissy."

Jane winced. Had they told him that she was a prude, too?

Because if he brought that up in front of Wyatt, she would happily just sink into the floor and try to disappear into the crevasses in the stone tile.

Wyatt shot his uncle a hard look. He might have even stepped on Leo's toe or something, because Leo gave a little yelp and eased away from both of them.

"Tell her you accept her apology," Wyatt insisted.

Leo turned to his nephew, chuckling as he asked. "She give you that shiner, boy?"

"Leo!"

"Okay, fine. I accept," he said, not looking either sincere or happy about being forced into saying it.

Wyatt didn't take his gaze off of his uncle. "Jane, would you excuse us, please? I'd like a moment alone with Leo."

"Of course," Jane conceded, eager to escape as fast as she could.

"What the hell is the matter with you?" Wyatt practically roared the moment Jane disappeared from sight.

"She is a prissy little thing. I still can't believe she hit me."

"She didn't hit you," Wyatt reminded him.

"But she meant to. The only thing that stopped her was you. And then she hit you."

Wyatt sighed, feeling a headache coming on, as it often did when he had to deal with Leo. "Did your doctor change your medication or something? Because you seem... particularly outrageous lately, even for you."

"I'm just enjoying myself here," Leo claimed, slapping his hands to his chest. "Life was meant to be enjoyed, boy."

"God help me," Wyatt muttered. "Are you trying to get kicked out of this place?"

"No, I love it here. This is the best old folks' home I've ever been in. Best-looking women, the friendliest, the fittest. I think this place is God's gift to Leo Gray."

"I doubt God sees it that way, and I know for a fact that Ms. Steele doesn't. She sees it as you potentially ruining this place, and she's this close to kicking you out." Wyatt held his thumb and his first finger an inch apart. "One more thing, and I swear, you're gone."

Leo made a disgusted, dismissive sound. "We done? 'Cause I'm supposed to meet someone in thirty minutes, and I need to spruce up a bit. A man can't just let himself go."

"Please tell me it's not one of Jane's relatives." Wyatt said, then wondered, would it be better or worse if it wasn't Kathleen or Gladdy?

"You gonna start policing my social calendar, boy?" Leo challenged.

Wyatt sighed. "There aren't enough hours in the day for me to control you."

Leo looked particularly pleased with himself. "Didn't think so."

"But I'm telling you, you're going to get kicked out of here, and Ms. Steele's going to blackball you with every retirement home administrator she knows, and she claims that will cover the entire state of Maryland. Think about it, Leo."

Jane found Gram and Gladdy in Gram's room whispering urgently to each other. They clammed up the minute they saw Jane.

That was odd.

"What are you two up to?" she asked.

Gram got a sad, disapproving look on her face. "Talking about you, my girl."

"We can't believe the things we're hearing, Jane. You attacked that sweet Leo Gray?"

"He is not sweet! He's trouble! How can you both not see that?"

"He is sweet as can be and just delightful to be around," Gram insisted. "Do you have any idea how boring most men in their eighties are? Sad and grumpy and complaining about one thing after another. Their backs, their head, their eyes. It's really disheartening what you have to choose from in men at our age, Jane."

"You could just give up on men altogether," Jane suggested.

Gram and Gladdy groaned, then looked at each other like it was too horrible an idea to even think about.

"Surely you've both had enough men by now," she tried.

"I hope to have a man in my life for as long as I'm breathing," Gram said.

Gladdy nodded her head, obviously agreeing. "You've just never learned how to truly enjoy a man, Jane. If you had, you'd understand."

"Enjoy a man?" She winced, remembering being called a prude and Gram and Gladdy feeling sorry for her, just because she didn't turn her life upside down for every man who showed the slightest interest in her. "I've had enjoyable men in my life before."

"Name one," Gladdy challenged her.

"I…uhhh…" She had to think, then came up with, "Andy Scovol. He was great fun. We did all sorts of things together, and I still miss him since he moved away."

"He was your best friend in fifth grade. That was eighteen years ago, and he wasn't a man. He was a boy. I bet you never even kissed him," Gram complained.

"Of course I didn't kiss him. He was my friend. It's okay to be friends with men, isn't it? Surely it's not all about sex."

Gladdy sighed. "Jane, we worry about you."

"And I worry about the two of you, too."

"Well, don't. We're fine."

"Fine," Gram agreed.

"But you won't be if you both keep running around with that man, Leo."

Gram gave a dismissive huff. "We told you. He's so much fun to have around."

"Well, you should know he's been having fun with both of you." There, she'd just blurted it out.

"Of course he has," Gram said. "We've had dinner together every day this week. We played doubles today in tennis, and we're going dancing downtown Saturday night."

"That's not all he's been doing." It had to be said, Jane knew. "I'm sorry, but it's not. His nephew says he's incapable of being faithful to any woman or of making any kind of long-term commitment."

Gladdy laughed. "Honey, we're both in our…seventies. How can a long-term commitment even apply at our age?"

Jane let the lying about their ages go. It wasn't the issue.

"He's been romancing you both. Gram, you think you're in love with him, and he was here, in this room…doing things with Gladdy yesterday."

Gladdy looked outraged.

"I'm sorry," Jane told her. "But he was."

"Doing…things?" Gram asked.

"Oh, pooh. I had something in my eye, and he was helping me get it out. I've already told Kathleen about it, and she understands perfectly. Don't you, Kathleen?"

"Of course I do." She patted Gladdy's hand with lifelong affection. "Gladdy and I would never let a man come between us."

"But...but you said you were in love with him." Jane tried.

"I'm quite sure I am. It's so exciting! Love at my age." She smiled like she didn't have a care in the world.

"See? I told you," Jane said to Gladdy. "Love. She thinks she's in love with that...cad!"

Gladdy rolled her eyes and said, "So what? Half the women at Remington Park are in love with Leo Gray. Jane, he's a wonderful man. I wish you could see that, and if I ever hear about you assaulting him again... Well, let's just say Kathleen and I are both greatly disappointed in you, Jane. Would you care to explain yourself?"

Jane frowned, her brow furrowing. *Everyone was in love with Leo?* That was it? That was their explanation?

Could she have completely misread the situation and thought Gram cared more about him than she actually did? Was no one's heart or lifelong friendship at risk here?

Jane sighed. It was hard work, taking proper care of two women in their eighties, especially two active, stubborn women who didn't want to be taken care of. "I just... I worry about the two of you."

"Well, we worry about you, too, Jane, darling," Gram said gently. "But we try not to overreact and let you live your own life, even if you're doing so in a way we disagree with at times."

"I'm...I'm sorry," Jane apologized, feeling ridiculous and so relieved.

Everything was okay. Nothing really bad was happening. She could relax, back off, never have to deal with Leo Gray again and maybe never see Wyatt again.

That was a good thing, wasn't it?

She felt vaguely disappointed and just…out of sorts. Which was silly, because this had to be a good thing.

Gladdy got up, came over to Jane, smiled down at her and gave her a little kiss on her forehead, like she used to do when Jane was little. "You're so sweet to fuss over us like this, but we're fine. Honestly. And I hate to rush off, but I made plans to meet a friend for bridge. Bye, darling. Bye, Kathleen."

"Bye," Jane whispered.

Gladdy left, and Jane for once relaxed that rigid posture of hers and fell back against her chair. "I'm so glad we got that cleared up."

But then she looked at Gram, and it appeared as if nothing at all had been cleared up, Gram's expression suggested that she had to tell Jane something and she was dreading it.

"What?" Jane asked.

Gram gave a shrug and a smile, then a sigh. "I just… Don't get upset, all right? You get upset over everything, Jane."

"Upset? Why would I get upset? You two said you're not fighting, that you haven't gone nuts over Leo Gray and that everything is fine. There's nothing upsetting about that. That's all good news. I'm happy. See? Happy Jane."

"The thing is, that isn't…entirely true," Gram confessed. "We haven't told Gladdy yet, although honestly, I don't believe it's going to be such a problem. I mean, I know she really likes Leo, but she hasn't said anything about being in love with him, and you know Gladdy. She doesn't do love."

"Neither do you," Jane said.

"Still…there's nothing official yet, but Leo and I've been talking, and… I'm fairly certain he's going to ask me to marry him! Jane, I'm just so happy, darling. Isn't it fabulous!"

Chapter Seven

"You can't do that," Jane said, after a long moment of stunned silence.

"Of course, we can. We can do anything we want."

"But…why would you want to?" Jane tried.

"Because that's what people in love do!" Gram gave her a huge, glowing smile.

Jane winced. Her head hurt. Her ears hurt. She could not listen to this anymore. She had no calm reasoning abilities left in her where Leo Gray was concerned.

"People in love do a lot of things," Jane said. *A lot of really stupid things.* "And you've only known him for two weeks, Gram."

"I know, but when it's right, Jane, you just know. This is right, and honestly, he's eighty-one—"

"No, honestly, he's eighty-six. He's lying about being eighty-one."

Gram laughed. "Well, I'm lying about being seventy-six, so I'd say we're even on that score."

"He was in Gladdy's room, necking with her just yesterday! That's what made me so mad! That's why I stormed off after him! Because he acted like it was nothing, to be messing around with you and her, like he could hurt you both and laugh about it."

"She said she had something in her eye, and I believe her, of course," Gram said sternly. "Now she may like him and enjoy spending time with him but she's not in love with him, and we'll all just sit down, talk this out and everything will be fine. You'll see."

"I don't think so, and I don't trust that man. You shouldn't, either."

"Things will be fine. Leo's going to tell her everything. Just wait and see."

Gladdy, just as Jane feared, was with Leo Gray!

When she finished with Gram, Jane went to the card room, where Gladdy wasn't, and then kept asking if anyone had seen her or Leo. She eventually tracked them down to a secluded bench near the tennis courts. Someone said it was a particularly favorite spot of Leo's to take his lady-friends.

Jane contemplated strangling him with her bare hands when she saw him and Gladdy sitting there, laughing hilariously, Gladdy's hand on his knee, Leo toying with a bit of Gladdy's long, pretty white hair.

Was the man on some new combination of Viagra and steroids?

This was ridiculous.

Jane crouched down behind a bush and tried to figure

out what to do next. It was like both Gram and Gladdy had completely lost all sense. Granted, they'd never been the most sensible women, but they hadn't been crazy, either.

Marry Leo Gray?

Gram would be safer jumping off a cliff.

He was like those wackos who founded cults and could get people to do anything he wanted, no matter how illogical or inherently dangerous.

Drink the Kook-Aid for Leo Gray.

And here was Jane, the only sensible one in the group. Well, maybe Wyatt was, too.

She had to see Wyatt again—and firmly ignored a little happy feeling that came along with that thought. There was simply no choice. He at least would help her.

She was getting ready to creep away from her hiding place behind the bush when Leo got up, kissed Gladdy on the cheek and headed Jane's way.

She gave a little yelp, fell to her knees and tried to crawl into the midst of the bushes. It was all the cover she could find that quickly, but it just wasn't big enough for hiding purposes. She was sure her butt was sticking out, and the stupid bush scratched her cheek, her arms, maybe even her ear and was likely ruining her pretty-yet-sensible, low-heeled pumps she'd just bought on sale.

Jane waited there, cuts stinging, knees sinking into the dirt, wondering how her life had been reduced to this—hiding in bushes—until she heard a man's voice.

"I'm telling you, there's something wrong with that little girl."

Leo, of course.

Groaning, even swearing under her breath in the bushes,

Jane couldn't bring herself to crawl out of there. It was too much. She had no dignity left, and Jane Carlton placed a great deal of value on her own sense of dignity. Every woman should, she believed. And hers was simply gone, all because of that man!

"You can come out now. He's gone," Gladdy said, sounding sad and worried herself.

Jane backed out on her hands and knees, then sat back on her heels, simply unable to look Gladdy in the eye.

"Honestly, Jane. Is there something going on that you're not telling us? Because you just aren't acting like yourself lately," Gladdy said.

"Of course I'm not acting like myself. I'm trying to save you and Gram from that man!"

"And we keep telling you, we don't need saving."

"Oh, yes, you do. Did he tell you what's really going on? What he did? What he and Gram are talking about?"

"Oh, please! What is going on? We're all going dancing together. We have dinner together. We just told you this. You remember, don't you, darling?"

"Of course I remember! There's nothing wrong with my memory! It's just…he's… I knew he wouldn't tell you. I just knew it."

"Tell me what?"

"About what's really going on here!" Jane was just all done in. She had dirt all over her knees and her new shoes, scratches on her face. She'd been caught hiding in a bunch of bushes, spying on her aunt, and two days ago, she'd nearly attacked an old man.

"Jane, everything's going to be fine. I'm sure of it. Kathleen and I are as happy as we've ever been. Life is very, very good."

"You're both crazy about the same man. This cannot end well!"

"Well, Leo will just have to pick one of us. Or... maybe not."

"Maybe not? What do you mean, maybe not?"

Gladdy hesitated, looking uneasy for once in the whole Leo Gray situation. "Jane, are you really sure you want me to answer that question? Because you have to think, before you ask some things, whether you really want to know the answers."

Jane shook her head. "What? What could I possibly not want to know?"

"Well...it wouldn't exactly be the first time Kathleen and I have...shared."

Jane got a funny feeling in the pit of her stomach. "Shared?"

Gladdy nodded.

"Shared...a man?"

"Yes," Gladdy whispered, a tiny smile on her pretty face.

When he got back to his office that afternoon, Wyatt got Leo's doctor on the phone. Wyatt was mostly getting the runaround about patient confidentiality and privacy laws, a thoroughly frustrating exchange.

"Look, he's just acting...funny," Wyatt finally said.

"Funny-sad or funny-odd?"

"He's definitely not sad, just...more stubborn about things," Wyatt explained. "And a little reckless."

"Ignoring what seem like perfectly reasonable requests?"

"Yes."

"And good advice from people trying to take care of him?"

"Exactly. What is that?"

"The most common complaint I hear from people trying to take care of older relatives," the doctor replied. "And unfortunately not a disease, as far as the medical profession has been able to identify."

Wyatt wanted to beat his head against his desk. "He's driving me crazy!"

"Me too, most of the time," the doctor admitted. "I can't get him to listen to a thing I say."

"Me either. What do we do?"

"Unfortunately, he's an adult, he's competent to make his own decisions—according to the law, at least—and he gets to go on making his own decisions until you can convince a court to find him incompetent."

Wyatt groaned.

"Look, you're always welcome to come with him to his appointments with me, if he'll let you, and then if you have concerns, I can try to play medical referee. If you're trying to look out for his health and safety, I'll back you up all the way. But I can't force him into anything."

"I feel like I'm the grown-up and he's the teenager," Wyatt complained. "Or maybe even a toddler."

"In my experience, most family members caring for older relatives feel that way eventually," the doctor sympathized. "Come to his next appointment. We'll talk."

Wyatt said he would, was just hanging up the phone with the doctor when his secretary buzzed, sounding agitated. "There's a woman here to see you."

"Lucy, I'm a fortunate man. There's almost always a woman here to see me," he spoke into the intercom.

"This one's different," Lucy claimed.

Wyatt shook his head. "Different, how?"

"She says she just crawled out of some bushes and she has to talk to you right now. It's about Leo."

Wyatt grinned broadly. Jane coming to him? This was a good day.

He opened the door, and then gaped at her.

She looked like a woman who'd been in a fight with a bush. There was a small twig of some kind sticking out of her hair, which was half falling down, half still in a droopy bun on her head. She had small scratches on her face and hands, leaves stuck to her skirt and bits of dirt clinging to her knees.

"Jane!" He went to her side, looking her over more carefully to make sure she wasn't really hurt. "What happened?"

"I hid in a bush," she said, as he took her hand and led her carefully into his office to a seat on his sofa. "Because I was spying on Leo and Gladdy, and then Leo left, and I didn't have time to really get out of the way. It was the bush or nothing. Not that it worked. They saw me anyway. And…I ended up like this."

"Lucy, would you get…anything you can find to help clean her up, please?" he called out the open office door, then turned to Jane, pulling stray leaves off her skirt, because that looked like the easiest place to start.

She looked so sad.

Wyatt carefully pulled the little twig out of her hair.

"Oops," she said. "I thought I got it all."

"It's fine now," Wyatt insisted, smoothing her hair back into place as best he could, which wasn't really all that well, but she didn't need to know that. He looked at her knees, dirt ground in, and asked, "You two didn't get into another fight, did you?"

"No," she responded meekly. "I refused to come out of hiding until he left."

Wyatt got an image of the scene in his mind, then said, "Good thinking, Jane."

Lucy returned with a damp cloth, and Wyatt gently cleansed the scratches on her face, which were red and angry looking but not deep.

"You poor thing," Lucy said, looking at Jane like she came from Mars or something.

She certainly wasn't Wyatt's usual type. He'd admit that. But it wasn't like she came from Mars, either. She was just...a little reserved, serious, all buttoned-up, although today's white blouse was coming untucked from her dark blue skirt in a couple of places.

"Lucy, will you run to the market on the corner and get some antibiotic ointment for these cuts?" Wyatt asked.

"No, it's okay," Jane said. "I can do that at home."

Wyatt shook his head. "You took care of me when I hurt my eye. I'm going to take care of you now."

That got Lucy's attention as she was walking out the office door. She'd been sure his black eye had something to do with a woman, and he'd refused to explain anything about it. Which made Lucy all the more curious. He gave her a curt nod to get out of there, then started cleaning up Jane's knees.

"So, do you think we're going to survive taking care of these three?" Wyatt asked, thinking he might at least get a smile out of Jane with that.

She looked even sadder. Her bottom lip started quivering. She sniffled once, then again. Tears filled her pretty blue-green eyes.

"No, no, no, don't do that," Wyatt begged.

He couldn't stand the idea of Jane crying. Not tough little Jane, who could handle anything. Her expression just crumbled. The harder she fought to control it, the more difficult it become.

Wyatt dabbed at the corner of her eyes with a tissue. "It's okay. Everything's fine. See? No need to cry."

Finally, she just blurted out, "Do you think I'm a prude?"

"No! My uncle called you a prude? I'll kill him—"

She shook her head, tears falling in earnest. "No, my aunt Gladdy did the other day, right before I ran into Leo and almost hit him. And I thought about it, but I didn't really think it was true. But today…today, I wasn't sure anymore."

Oh, God.

What had Leo done? What had Jane seen from those bushes to have her thinking she was a prude?

Ooh. Ick. This was like teenagers walking in on their parents having sex.

Jane was sobbing now, and Wyatt was thinking he probably wouldn't be too out of line if he just kissed her until she stopped. It wasn't as if he'd had many opportunities to grab Jane and kiss her, when he didn't think she'd maybe slap him for trying. But she was genuinely distressed now and kissing was a great distraction, he reasoned. Maybe taking advantage of the situation, just a little, but he felt certain he could stop her crying, and that was what was important. Wasn't it?

Poor thing had been attacked by a bush, called a prude and seen God-only-knows-what that had left her in this condition. Serious comforting was in order, Wyatt calculated.

He took a seat beside her and then just lifted her onto his lap.

Her eyes flew wide open, and she looked at him as if she wasn't quite sure what was up and that she might need to protest. He'd been right to be wary. Kissing her right now was not a good idea.

"It's okay, Jane," he said softly, then urged her to let herself lean on him, put her head on his shoulder.

She sat ramrod straight on his lap, stubborn to the core and resisting with all she had. She might just tell him she didn't need comforting, and if she tried that, it would be all he could do not to laugh. It would be such a ridiculous assertion, but he could imagine Jane trying to make it.

"Just for a minute," he suggested. "I won't tell. If anybody ever asks, you're the toughest woman I know. I'll swear to it."

She sniffled again and finally, ever-so-slowly, settled herself against him, her head falling to his shoulder, her sobs leaving her whole body shaking.

Wyatt closed his eyes and let his face find its way to her hair, inhaling the scent that was Jane, taking in the warmth of her body, the softness of her, the satisfaction of finally having her in his arms.

He was going to get her on her back on this couch and kiss her before this was over. He promised himself. As soon as she stopped crying.

So he stroked her hair, her back, promised her that everything was going to be okay. That he would handle anyone who said mean things to her and make it clear that they were never to treat her badly again.

Her head popped up off his shoulder and she sat up straight on his lap again. "I can't believe they called me that name!"

"I know," he agreed. "I'm sorry."

"That's one of those awful labels people use against

women, to try to rob them of their power by taking a dig
at their femininity. It's patently unfair. Especially when it
comes from another woman. Especially a woman who's
supposed to love me!"

A woman? Well, at least it wasn't Leo. But still...

"Your grandmother?"

"No, Gladdy."

"She loves you, Jane. You know she does. She's
just...old, and it's like old people think that their age
comes with the right to be as outrageous, as demanding and
as stubborn as they please."

"Yes! I take care of her and Gram. I try really hard to take
good care of them, and be a good girl. I mean...a woman.
A good, responsible, hard-working, intelligent woman."

"You are. You're all those things."

"And what do they do? They insult me and try to
demean me with that word!"

"They should be ashamed of themselves. Do you want
me to try to make them ashamed? Because I will," he
promised. He could shame sweet, little old ladies for Jane.

"I don't think you could. I don't think anyone could. I
don't think they have any shame. They never have!"

He hated asking. Really, he did, but he figured he had
to know, because he was still afraid Leo had something to
do with this. "So...Jane...what happened, exactly? To
make you so upset today."

She looked too embarrassed to tell him.

This was going to be bad. Really bad.

"It was about...picking and choosing," she said finally.
"Or...actually...not picking and choosing. Leo not having
to pick between them, because...well, first, Gram said he had
chosen her and that he was going to tell Gladdy everything.

But he didn't, and when I tried to tell Gladdy instead, she said maybe he would choose, but maybe he wouldn't have to."

Wyatt shook his head. "Because Gladdy doesn't want him anymore?"

"No, because Gram and Gladdy might…share."

Wyatt figured he must not have heard her right. Or understood.

"Share…?" And then he got it. No, surely he hadn't gotten it. "Share…Leo?"

Jane nodded, looking truly horrified.

Yeah, this was bad.

"You mean…" Wyatt had really disturbing pictures of sharing in his mind. "Take turns with him? One gets him one night and another…the other? Like on a schedule or something?"

"I don't know," Jane cried, looking pitiful and sad again.

"Like they'd really put up with him going from one bed to the other?"

Jane pressed her hands over her ears. "I don't know! I really don't want to know!"

"God, neither do I," Wyatt agreed. "That man's eighty-six! Something like this could kill him."

"I would think so!" Jane whimpered.

"Your aunt really said something about her and your Gram…sharing Leo?" Wyatt couldn't quite take it in.

Jane nodded. "She said it wouldn't be the first time!"

"With…they've already…shared Leo?" Oh, please, don't let it be that, Wyatt thought. He couldn't take it. It was too much.

"No. It was another man. Years ago. During the war. I'm not even sure which war. I was too horrified to ask. But apparently, there was a war on, men were scarce and they were lonely. This man showed up and they liked him, but they didn't love him or anything like that, and he stayed around for a while, and they...shared. It worked, Gladdy said. Got them all through a difficult time, and... I don't know. That's what she said."

"Damn, the women in your family are just full of surprises," Wyatt said.

Jane nodded, then started whimpering again. "Sharing? I mean, is this what modern women are putting up with these days, and calling it a sex life?"

"Not the ones I know," Wyatt assured her.

"Either that or... I mean, don't tell me that he's not going back and forth, because they're all... You don't think they're all in that bed together, do you?" she cried, tears falling once again. "Surely that's not what they meant!"

Wyatt shook his head. "No way. Not at eighty-six—"

"Even with drugs?"

"I don't think any drug is that good," he tried to reassure her.

"Because I would never do that, Wyatt. No way. If that means I'm a prude, so be it. I'll be a prude. But I just can't do that."

"I promise, you don't have to do that." He would never ask her to share, or to take part in any kind of sharing, except the one-man, one-woman kind of sharing. Jane would be plenty enough woman for him, he decided.

"I just..." She sniffed, looking thoroughly defeated. "I'm not the most...adventurous woman. I know that. I'm cautious. I'm careful. I admit that, but I'm not some kind of sexual dinosaur, either! At least, I didn't think so. Until now."

"Oh, Jane. I'm so sorry," he said, tucking her head to

his chest once again. Poor thing. She was just over-whelmed by the hijinks of three sexually adventurous, eighty-something-year-olds.

Who wouldn't be?

Wyatt let her cry a bit longer, rubbing her back, stroking her hair, trying to be a gentleman, promising that this would be okay somehow.

He really hated to see her this upset, especially about that ugly word—*prude*. He was fairly certain she wasn't a prude. And even if she did have some…prudish tenden-cies, he was sure he could fix those, that they couldn't withstand the kind of effort Wyatt Gray was willing to put forth on her behalf.

An effort he was eager to extend for Jane.

He just wasn't sure if she'd be happy about that or call him names in return, and he was seldom so uncertain with any woman. But this was Jane, and Jane was different. He tried patience, more soothing, more gentlemanly behavior, and then, when he wasn't sure he could stand it any longer, she finally stopped crying.

And then, finally, he kissed her.

Chapter Eight

One minute, Jane was devastated, thinking she was a prude and just unable to get the image of all that sharing out of her mind, and the next, she was lying flat on her back on the couch with Wyatt stretched on top of her, kissing her.

Not grabbing her, mauling her, rushing her. Just kissing her. Lazily, luxuriously, longingly. Jane wasn't sure she'd ever been kissed like that before.

He tasted like cinnamon and coffee. Sweet. A wicked little zing that rattled around her whole body from head to toe. His lips were the softest things she'd ever felt and he smelled glorious, and the weight of his big, hard body on top of hers, the heat, the power…

Jane did not feel like a prude at all.

She did exactly what she wanted to in that moment— something she had seldom wanted to do in her life with a man. She opened herself to him completely, throwing herself into the moment, kissing him back, feeling her heart pound and her body go limp. He had a hand in her hair, tearing it down from what was left of her hairdo after her tangle with the bush. He freed her hair and then stroked through it, holding the side of her face in one hand, nuzzling his nose against her ear. Then his mouth found the sensitive hollow of her throat, her neck.

She arched against him, heard him groan, thought about how she could just happily dissolve into a puddle in his arms, and let him do whatever he wanted to with her. Just like that.

His mouth came back to hers, and she felt his thrusting tongue. Jane thought about taking him into her body in another way. Heat pooled between her legs. A pulse throbbed. He wanted her, too. His body told her so as he rocked gently against her.

It was as if every sexual thought Jane had ever had came roaring to life, right here in this room, on Wyatt's couch.

"I am not a prude," she said proudly.

He lifted his head a fraction of an inch, grinned down at her. "No, you most certainly are not."

He started kissing her again.

It felt glorious, sweet and wicked at the same time, overwhelming.

And then Jane remembered—they were in Wyatt's office, in the middle of the afternoon. His secretary was coming back to give Jane first aid for her skirmish with the bush at Remington Park.

The bush, Leo, Gladdy, Gram, sharing…

Jane pushed Wyatt away. "I can't do this."

"Why not?" he asked, holding himself up on his elbows, but still stretched out on top of her.

"Your secretary's coming back with first aid supplies, remember?"

"No. Not until you reminded me."

"And besides, I don't have sex with men on the sofas in their offices," she said, then feared she was sounding prudish again.

Did women often have sex with men in their offices? Was that a requirement of non-prudishness, too?

"Am I supposed to?" she asked.

"Supposed to what?" Wyatt questioned, carefully climbing off her and sitting on the edge of the sofa.

"Have sex with men on their sofas?"

"Not unless you want to," he told her, running his hands through his hair, hair she thought she might have mussed up herself a moment ago.

Jane sighed. It was all so bewildering. What was normal and what was not? What was expected? In her admittedly not abundant experience, men wanted a lot these days. They expected a lot. Quickly. Very quickly.

"I'm sorry," she said.

He frowned. "Why? You're right. Lucy is coming back. I told her to. And I know you're not the kind of woman who'd be comfortable having sex in my office on a sofa during business hours."

She got worried. "But does that—"

"That doesn't make you anything except who you are, Jane, and there's nothing wrong with who you are. Any man who tries to tell you there is is an ass and probably just out to get whatever he can get as fast as he can."

"But you… I know you… I suspect you…wouldn't really have a problem with…something like this."

He shrugged. "Maybe every now and then, for something quick and different. But the thing I like best…is someplace totally quiet and private, no time constraints at all, no interruptions. And nothing to do with sharing."

"Really?" she asked in wonder.

He nodded.

"Oh." She was thinking about pulling him back down on top of her on the couch. He knew it, too. She could tell by that flare of heat in his eyes as he watched her watching him.

She sighed, took his tie in her hand and gave it a tug. Grinning like the no-doubt wicked man he was, he happily lowered his mouth to hers once again. If she was going to be wicked herself, she might as well start right now with the time they had until his secretary did get back.

"You're just trying to mess with me now," he said stopping with his lips a breath away from hers.

"Yes," she admitted.

"You know Lucy's coming back, and you know I know, so you think you're perfectly safe here with me. That I'm not going to really do anything."

"Yes," she agreed.

"That is so bad of you, Jane," he said, still not kissing her. "And you're supposed to be such a good girl."

She'd been watching his eyes, his mouth, waiting for it to descend that last inch and kiss her again, and she hadn't been paying attention to anything else. It wasn't until she felt cool air on her chest that she realized he'd unbuttoned her blouse.

He took the tip of his nose and skimmed it along the line of her bra as it rose and fell over her breasts, nudging it aside here and there. Then he started playing with her skin with his tongue, his warm breath heating her nipples as he got closer and closer to them.

She gasped, ran a hand into his hair and grabbed on, trying to pull him away, but in the end, not having the will.

He nibbled on her collarbone, on the side of her neck. She just melted when he did that to her neck and was starting to rethink the whole sex-in-the-office thing.

Who would ever really know? Jane could be quiet. At least, she always had been, before Wyatt. She didn't think Wyatt would be particularly quiet, though, and honestly, she wasn't sure she could be.

She was whimpering already.

"Can you be quiet?" she asked him. "Really quiet?"

He jerked back, just enough to stare down at her, as if he couldn't believe she had just said that. "No, but I can throw you over my shoulder and haul you out of here. I live right down the street. We can be in my bed in ten minutes flat."

She got a little scared then.

He laughed. "Didn't think so."

Oh, she'd ruined it! "I'm sorry."

"I'm not. I don't think you're quite ready for this, Jane. And I can wait."

"Really?"

"Well, I don't want to, but I'm capable of it. I'm actually looking forward to talking you into it."

"Talking?" she asked, not feeling so bad after all.

He grinned. "Whatever it takes."

He nearly had her blouse off by the time Lucy got back, because Jane did feel safe, she was truly enjoying herself and they couldn't seem to keep their hands off each other and honestly, why should they?

Lucy just waltzed right in, saying, "I got antibiotic cream and… Oh, sorry. I—"

Jane gave a little yelp, face flaming. She really had forgotten, there at the end, exactly where they were.

"It's okay, Lucy," Wyatt said, sitting up and keeping his broad back to her.

Jane couldn't see her, and she figured that meant Lucy couldn't see Jane as she buttoned up her blouse, wondering just how many times Lucy had walked in on a scene like this between her boss and some woman.

No, she wasn't going to think like that. She would just think about Wyatt and that wonderful mouth of his, those talented hands, the way he smelled, the wicked things he made her want to do.

"I'll just leave this stuff right here and leave you two alone," Lucy said, then whispered to Wyatt. "You know, your door has a lock on it."

"Sorry, Luce."

But he didn't look sorry. He looked like a man who was very happy with himself. Of course, why wouldn't he be?

"I bet you get every woman you want," Jane said, not upset, not mad, just…marveling that she could ever actually think about getting involved with a man like him. Even if it was nothing but sex. Great sex.

Surely a woman was allowed to have one highly satisfying, purely sexual relationship in her life. She'd decided Wyatt would be hers.

"You really want to talk about me and other women, Jane?"

"No, actually, I don't."

He nodded. "Good. I'd rather talk about you and me. Have dinner with me tomorrow night. I've been dying to see you in something other than one of those little power suits."

"You don't like my suits?"

"I do. I think they're adorable, which I know isn't the image you're going for. But I can't help it. You're just so cute."

"You're sounding less desirable to me with every word that comes out of your mouth," she warned.

"Because I like the way you dress?"

"Because I am not cute. Kittens are cute. Puppies are cute. Little girls are cute—"

"So I guess you wouldn't consider dressing up as a Catholic schoolgirl for me? Or maybe in a cheerleader outfit?"

Her mouth fell open, and she was just about to get really mad when he burst out laughing at her.

"You rat!"

"I like grown women, Jane. I have no doubt that you are one. And now that I think about it, wear one of your little suits. I always see you that way in my head, anyway. I think they're really sexy."

"Well, in that case, I wouldn't dream of dressing in any way other than to please you, the man."

"Hey, it was a compliment."

She'd gotten her blouse buttoned up and tucked back into her skirt. "I have to go. I have to get some work done, especially if I'm not working late tomorrow night, because I'm having dinner with you."

He handed her the bag of first-aid supplies Lucy had brought back from the store and said, "You're really not going to let me play doctor?"

"I don't think that would be wise," she said, heading for the door, not quite able to believe what she'd already done today with him or what he might expect after the obligatory dinner date tomorrow night.

He watched her go, stopping her just as she reached for

the door handle, his body wrapping itself around hers, trapping her between him and the door.

"Maybe one of those suits without any underwear? What do you say, Jane?"

"That you're crazy."

He dropped a little kiss on her cheek and then backed up and let her go.

Lainie stared at Jane when she walked into the office an uncharacteristic hour and fifteen minutes later than expected.

"What?" Jane asked. "Was I humming?"

Or grinning like a woman who'd nearly had sex with Wyatt in his office, or one who was contemplating all the sinful behavior she might partake with him the very next evening?

"Did you get mugged?" Lainie asked.

"Oh!" Jane touched the scratches on her face and grinned. "I forgot. I hid in a bush."

Lainie looked skeptical. "Why?"

"Because there was no other place to hide," Jane explained.

"Does this have something to do with that man? The amazingly reasonable one?"

"Oh, I don't think he's all that reasonable, really. He's actually…"

Outrageous. Wicked. Gorgeous. Jane sighed happily, then remembered where she was. "I can't talk about him now. I'm so far behind, and I need to get out of here early tomorrow. I have a date."

"A date? With him?"

Jane nodded.

"Has he...done something to you?" Lainie prodded, looking worried.

"Done something?"

"Drugged you, maybe? You're really not acting like yourself, Jane. You haven't been since you met him. And there are all sorts of things men can put into drinks these days to get women to do anything they want. This is serious."

"Wyatt Gray's never had to drug a woman in his life. They probably line up for the chance to give him what he wants."

"And that doesn't...infuriate you?"

Jane thought about it. At one point, it would have. She knew that. But it seemed she'd discounted the whole bit about what the women might want in this situation. Women could be taken advantage of, certainly, and they often were. Jane knew from experience with the women who came to her seminars. But she didn't think Wyatt took advantage of women. She thought he just enjoyed them, and they enjoyed him.

She wanted to enjoy him and very much wanted him to enjoy her.

"I think I may have been a little harsh in my judgments about men," she admitted.

Lainie started dropping things, everything she was carrying, actually. A coffee mug, some papers, little pink message slips for Jane. Flustered, she hurried to pick them up, then looked at Jane as if she'd grown three heads in the last five seconds.

"What has that man done to you?" she asked.

"I know most men are jerks. Believe me, I do. It's just that, not all of them are. There must be some decent men out there. Some who can be trusted in...certain... limited...situations."

"You want to go to bed with him," Lainie guessed.

Jane felt heat coming into her cheeks. "I'm allowed to have a sex life—"

"I know. You just never have before. Not in all the time I've known you, I bet."

Jane clamped her mouth shut, thinking back to exactly when she'd hired Lainie. Had it been that long? She wasn't going to answer that.

"Just be careful, okay? I don't want to see you get hurt," Lainie said.

"I won't. I know exactly what I'm getting into. I certainly know that nothing lasting will ever come out of this, and that I'm not his usual type, which has made him more interested than he'd normally be. But I know that in the end, we'll just go our separate ways, and that'll be it."

"And you're fine with that?"

She sighed. "I wouldn't say fine with that, but I'm an adult, and like you said, I get lonely at times. Wyatt's here, and I'm here, and he's…he's…he's the sexiest man I've ever met in my life, Lainie. I'm thinking about going to dinner with him in one of my power suits with no underwear. Does that sound…normal?"

"Not for you," Lainie yelped.

"No, I mean for a woman not like me. A woman who likes men. Really likes them. And really likes sex. For that kind of woman. Would that kind of woman do that?"

Lainie sighed. "Jane, are you sure he didn't drug you? Maybe I should come along on this date, just to make sure he doesn't…that he isn't…you know? A bad guy. Or we could run a background check on him. You have that friend on the police force. Just in case. How about that? A background check and a credit check. You can't be too careful."

"Yes, you can. I've been careful too long. And I'm done with it," Jane declared.

She was going to dinner without her underwear, after all.

Chapter Nine

The next afternoon Jane skipped out on much of the work she'd hoped to accomplish. Her heart just wasn't in it. She went home and took a bath instead. A nice, long, sexy soak, because she wanted to smell good all over.

The no-panties thing had been just a crazy idea at first, but Lainie had been so sure Jane had become demented or perhaps incapacitated by drugs someone had slipped her, that Jane had been insulted a bit. Granted, it wasn't like her to ever do that, but surely it wasn't completely out of the realm of possibility.

It was like the odds of her winning the lottery, maybe. Not probable, but not impossible.

She decided she was going to do it.

It's not as if it would kill her, and no one would ever have to know. It wasn't as if she'd promised to hop in bed with Wyatt tonight, even though she suspected he was fairly certain she would. And at this moment, she wanted to. But if later she got too nervous, too scared, or changed her mind, she didn't have to, and if she did, her pantyless state could very well go undetected.

It could be her wicked little secret.

Jane was not as stuffy or prudish as anyone thought. She liked that idea. That it was more like a dare she'd given herself, something she wanted to prove to herself.

Opening up her closet door, she frowned at row after row of power suits, all virtually identical except for their color. Was she really that boring? That predictable? It was just so easy this way. Buy good-quality suits that didn't go out of style, pick a color, pair it with a white blouse and she was ready to go, day after day.

Jane sighed. Wyatt had asked her to wear one.

She picked the brightest color she had—a hot, candy-pink—then got to all those white blouses. It was definitely not a buttoned-up, white-blouse kind of night, either.

In her underwear drawer, she picked up lace camisole after lace camisole. Jane wasn't a busty woman, and she wasn't going to endure a stuffed or even water-filled bra to try to make her look bustier every day, just to please some man who only wanted to look at her chest. But she did like camisoles with a little support that doubled as soft, comfortable bras. They were pretty, and some were even soft and pretty at the same time. Truth be told, she felt a bit sexy in those little camisoles. She just always wore her buttoned-up blouses over them.

Tonight…maybe she'd skip the blouse and wear one of her prettiest camisoles instead.

She found one in white satin, the neckline made of lace trim and cut straight across, so it didn't look like a bra or underwear necessarily. She slipped it on, thinking it certainly felt a little wicked against her skin.

Pulling on the slightly cropped jacket to her suit and buttoning the two buttons, she thought it looked sexy. She was showing some skin, but nothing outrageous, as long as she didn't take off her jacket.

She gave herself a pep talk that she could indeed do this, slipped off the jacket and then put on a robe, so she could take the time to do her hair and put on a little makeup, saving the panties or no-panties decision until the last possible minute.

Her hands actually shook as she put on mascara.

Why did women do this to themselves? Get so worked up over a man? She found lotion, to match the scent she'd used in her bath, smoothed it over her skin around and even beneath the camisole. Which had her thinking of Wyatt's hands under there, touching her everywhere.

Jane frowned, watching the clock move ever closer to the appointed time of their date. It wasn't as if the man was going to push his way into her apartment and strip her naked the moment he arrived.

At least, she didn't think so.

Maybe she could call Lainie and ask if…that might be something she should be prepared for, although how a woman prepared for someone like Wyatt to do something like that to her…

She set the bottle of lotion down, dropping the cap as she tried to put it back on. Maybe she should have a drink, and not a white wine spritzer.

He was just a man, she kept telling herself. Reasonable in some things perhaps, more good-looking than most, kind to his elderly uncle, but beyond that, just a man. She was probably all worked up over nothing.

▶ If offer card is missing write to: The Reader Service, P.O. Box 1867, Buffalo, NY 14240-1867 or visit www.ReaderService.com ▶

NO POSTAGE
NECESSARY
IF MAILED
IN THE
UNITED STATES

BUSINESS REPLY MAIL
FIRST-CLASS MAIL   PERMIT NO. 717   BUFFALO, NY

POSTAGE WILL BE PAID BY ADDRESSEE

THE READER SERVICE
PO BOX 1867
BUFFALO NY 14240-9952

I accept your offer!

Please send me two free
Silhouette Special Edition® novels
and two mystery gifts (gifts
worth about $10). I understand
that these books are completely
free—even the shipping and
handling will be paid—and I am
under no obligation to purchase
anything, ever, as explained on the
back of this card.

**About how many NEW paperback fiction books have you
purchased in the past 3 months?**

❑ 0-2	❑ 3-6	❑ 7 or more
E4LM	**E4LX**	**E4MA**

235/335 SDL

Please Print

FIRST NAME

LAST NAME

ADDRESS

APT.#   CITY

STATE/PROV.   ZIP/POSTAL CODE

**Visit us online at
www.ReaderService.com**

▲ Detach card and mail today. No stamp needed. ▲

S-SE-03/10

Her doorbell rang.

Jane yelped, practically jumping out of her skin.

He was a full nine minutes early!

She dropped the robe, grabbed her skirt and put it on, along with the jacket and buttoned up. She'd never put on her panties, and she was feeling incredibly, sinfully bare, but looking in the mirror...

No one would ever have to know, she told herself as he rang the doorbell again and she went to answer it.

Wyatt stopped in the doorway and stared, a slow smile coming across his face.

"Pink is a great color on you, Jane."

She stood absolutely still, feeling cool silk and lace against her breasts and, down there, nothing but a slight breeze coming up her short, straight-cut skirt.

He reached out, letting his fingertips skim along the lace neckline of the camisole, his eyes dark and smoky looking. "If this is underwear, I've changed my mind. I approve."

"It's not underwear," she claimed. Not really. "It's a camisole top."

"Pretty," he said appreciatively.

He looked good enough to eat, she thought, in his sleek, dark, perfectly fitted suit. But he didn't needed to hear it. And given the look in his eyes, she really didn't trust him not to push her down on the couch and start taking her clothes off, right here and now.

"I'm starving," she said, taking him by the arm and steering him toward the front door. "We should go."

"Whatever you want, Jane. I intend to be a perfect gentleman tonight."

"I don't believe that for a second," she told him.

But she got him out the door, into his car and on the way to the restaurant. Jane leaned back in the soft leather seats of his sleek, roomy Mercedes, and tried to relax as he drove just a tad fast for her tastes, but seemingly in perfect control.

It was just dinner, she told herself.

His cell phone rang. He took it out of his pocket, glanced at the number, then clicked it off. "Sorry. Meant to do that before I picked you up."

"It's all right. Mine's not turned off, either, now that I think about it."

She fished it out of her purse, where it had been buried under everything and saw that she had three missed calls, including two from Ms. Steele while she'd been in the tub.

"Uh, oh. Was yours from Ms. Steele?"

Wyatt nodded. "But we're not going to think about her tonight. Tonight is for us."

"I know, but…she called me twice, which doesn't really bother me, but Amy, the sweet aide who's such a great cook, she called, too, and she never calls me."

"Jane, if you want to call her, go ahead."

"If I don't call, I'll spend all night wondering what's wrong." She hid the redial button and waited until Amy came on the line. "Amy, it's Jane. Is everything all right?"

"Jane, I'm so glad it's you. Do you…know where Kathleen is?"

"She's not at the cottage?"

"As far as we can tell, she's not anywhere at Remington Park. She missed her regular tennis lesson and we started looking for her. Then we figued out that Mr. Gray's missing, too. They didn't say anything to you about…taking off for a few days, did they?"

"No. What about Gladdy? She must know."

"We're looking for her right now, but I thought you might know what's going on or that, if you didn't, you'd want to know. We can't find Kathleen."

"We'll be right there," she told Amy. "Uh… I'm with Mr. Gray's nephew, so you don't have to call him. I'll fill him in. See you in a few minutes."

Wyatt groaned as she got off the phone. "Don't tell me."

"They can't find Leo or my grandmother. They're canvassing the whole place to find Gladdy right now, hoping she knows where they are."

Jane groaned unhappily. She'd so been looking forward to an evening with Wyatt, even if the prospect did scare her a bit.

"Can we throw uncle Leo into a dungeon in chains when we find him?"

"I wouldn't tell on you if you did." Jane sighed. "So, where does he like to take his women?"

"All sorts of places, but he doesn't drive anymore. It was a battle, but we finally got rid of his car. Does Kathleen still drive?"

Jane nodded. "Not often, but she does. She and Gladdy keep a car at Remington Park that they share. Gram and Leo could be anywhere by now."

They got to her grandmother and Gladdy's cottage to find it in an uproar of worried older women, a few security guards and Ms. Steele in full-battle mode, questioning a withering Amy, who looked as if she just wanted to hide.

At the sight of Wyatt, Ms. Steele made a face that actually scared Jane a bit. Amy came running over to her, whispering, "She wants to fire me, Jane, and I didn't do anything wrong. I swear."

Jane eased around to put her body between Amy and Ms. Steele. She'd protect Amy. So would Wyatt.

The administrator puffed up her chest and glared in their direction. "So, the two of you have no idea where Mr. Gray and Ms. Carlton might be?"

"No," Wyatt said.

"Neither said anything to you about going away for a few days?" she grilled them.

"Nothing," Wyatt insisted.

"What about Gladdy?" Jane tried. "Gram would never take off without telling Gladdy where she was going."

"We still have people looking for her," Amy said.

"Did you look in Gram's room? Are any of her things missing?" Jane continued.

"I looked, but I really wasn't sure if she'd taken some things or not. But her big suitcase is there," Amy offered.

"There's a smaller matching one, something made to fit under a seat on an airplane. What about that?"

"I didn't see it."

Jane headed for Gram's room, Wyatt and Amy following her. At first glance, it looked as if everything was in place. Jane opened the top two drawers. They hadn't been cleaned out, but Amy was right. It was impossible to tell if Gram had packed for, say…a few days.

She opened the closet, saw the big suitcase, pulled it out and unzipped it.

Empty.

"She keeps the smaller bag inside the big one, to save space," Jane said.

She did a quick sweep of the room looking for the

smaller bag anyway. Wyatt helped, shaking his head when he came up empty.

"So, she's gone," Jane said.

They searched the grounds and Gladdy's room for another twenty minutes before Ms. Bea, one of the residents of the cottage, woke up from her nap and came out of her room to hear that Kathleen was missing.

"Oh, my goodness. I had no idea you were all looking for her," Ms. Bea said. "She gave me a note to give you, Jane, as she was rushing out the door this afternoon."

The lady pulled out a familiar envelope in light yellow—Gram's signature stationery—and handed it to Jane.

Tearing it open, Jane read:

My Darling Jane,
Please don't be upset. I know you think this is wrong, but I'm absolutely certain it's right, and at our age, Leo and I simply don't have time to waste. I hate that you won't be there for the ceremony, but we'll be back in a few days and have our own little family celebration then.
All my love,
Gram

Wyatt, reading over her shoulder, swore softly and shook his head.

"Eloped?" Jane yelled, then turned to glare at Wyatt. "They've eloped?"

"No. Leo wouldn't do that. He absolutely promised me that he would never get married again without letting me take care of the prenup," he claimed. "I've cleaned up too many messes of his before, after the fact, but never again. He swore to me."

"Gram, too," Jane admitted. "I made her promise the same thing. She actually has an investment portfolio thanks to me. I worked hard to make sure she'll always be taken care of financially, and she promised she wouldn't put it at risk."

Wyatt smiled at her admiringly, then took her face in his hands and gave her a quick, deep, satisfying kiss. "There you go. That's my girl. Woman, I mean. What a woman!"

He let her go, as if he might have forgotten where they were, or that he'd been surprised by the impulse to grab her and kiss her that way.

Jane looked around, seeing Gram and Gladdy's friends in the cottage beaming at them. Amy, too. Ms. Steele, on the other hand, looked at Jane as if Jane had surely lost her mind, no doubt thinking all the Gray men were troublemakers.

"So," Wyatt said, sounding very lawyerly once again. "We can hope they remember their promises to both of us and don't go through with this. Or that we can find them in time to stop them."

"How can we find them?" Jane asked. "We have no idea where they went."

"If they've run off to get married, they're headed for Vegas."

"How do you know?" Jane asked.

"Leo always gets married in Vegas," he stated, as if it was some kind of unwritten law.

"Sentimental, is he?" Jane guessed.

"Not so much about marriage, but about the city and this one little chapel on the strip, yes. What is that place called? It's an Elvis song."

"Doesn't every hurry-up wedding chapel in Vegas have something to do with an Elvis song?"

"'Love Me Tender.' That's it," Wyatt confirmed. "The Love Me Tender Wedding Chapel."

"Oh, this is so exciting!" Ms. Bea said. "So romantic."

No, Jane thought, *really, it's not.*

It was foolish, crazy and completely irresponsible. Gram barely knew the man, and Gladdy… What about Gladdy?

"We have to find Gladdy," she remembered.

They searched Gladdy's room again, and finally, there in her jewelry box was a little note addressed to Jane.

Jane, Darling,
I know you'll fret. Honestly, Jane, you fret too much. But Leo, Kathleen and I are going away for a few days by ourselves. Don't worry. Everything will be fine. Leo and I are going to explain it all to Kathleen, and I'm sure when we do, she'll understand. Leo and I can't help how we feel about each other, Jane. He's the most wonderful man. To think, when I come back, I'll be a married woman again!
All my love,
Gladdy

Jane let the note fall from her hand, simply unable to hold on to it any longer.

Beside her, Wyatt just said, "No, no way! He's not crazy. Irritating and infuriating, but not crazy."

"He's eloping with two women?" Jane fumed. "How does any sane man elope with two women? What does he think he's going to do? Make up his mind when they get there, and both women will put up with that? Give him whichever one he wants?"

"I don't know," Wyatt admitted. "It doesn't make any sense."

"Or maybe he's just going to marry them both!" Jane theorized, horrified. "Maybe he thinks he can get away with bigamy, too."

Wyatt actually looked hopeful at that.

"What could possibly be good about a man committing bigamy?" she countered.

"It would invalidate both marriages," Wyatt said, shrugging apologetically. "We wouldn't have to worry about the prenup thing."

"Oh, well, I suppose that's one good thing." And then she got mad all over again. "Wyatt, he's going to break their hearts! He thinks he can have both of them, and he's bound to break their hearts. We have to stop him!"

"I know, Jane. I'm so sorry. I've already called my travel agent. I got us two seats on the last plane out tonight to Vegas, but we have to get to the airport right now."

They made it.

Barely.

No luggage or anything, but they made the plane, settling into two seats in the very last row of first class only moments before the plane backed out of the gate.

Jane hadn't done anything so impulsive as flying off to Vegas at the drop of a hat in years, and she hated to admit it—given the fact that Gram and Gladdy were going to get their hearts broken—but she was a little excited about the whole crazy trip.

And to be making it with Wyatt. He really was a very nice man, even if his uncle was a troublesome, potentially crazy womanizer. She actually wished she had hit the old man with her briefcase now. But none of that was Wyatt's fault. She'd been looking forward to their date tonight, but she supposed a lunatic, last-minute trip to Vegas together was even better.

Date, she remembered. Something about the date, she was forgetting.

What? And then she got it.

Oops.

"What's wrong?" Wyatt asked.

"I just remembered. I'm not wearing any panties."

Chapter Ten

Wyatt was certain he could not have possibly heard her right.

Jane with no panties?

"What?" he repeated.

She leaned over to him this time, whispering urgently. "I'm not wearing any panties."

He looked down at her hot-pink suit, the color that had him thinking of tropical islands, the blazing sun, gleaming tanned skin and Jane. She came alive completely in that color.

And if that weren't bad enough, from the moment he'd opened the door to her apartment and seen her there, he'd been trying to figure out exactly what kind of top she was wearing.

Because it looked like underwear.

The cropped jacket of her hot-pink suit, buttoned with

two buttons at the bottom and open in a wide, deep V-neck to show off… Well, it really looked like underwear.

A lady's camisole was underwear, wasn't it?

Silky and lacy and one of those tricky fabrics that was part white flowers and part…sheer. A really unfair trick that had him thinking what he was seeing was, for all intents and purposes, bare skin. But he couldn't be sure. Maybe he was, maybe he wasn't.

It was just enough to drive him crazy.

Especially seeing it on Jane.

Buttoned-up-to-here Jane.

And now she claimed that under that pencil-slim, hot-pink skirt that stopped a couple of lovely inches above her lovely knees, she wasn't wearing any panties?

He stared at her waist, her hips, as if he could see through the fabric and find the answer. She'd turned in her seat, angling her body toward his, and the skirt was riding up even higher on the outside of her right thigh, but not nearly high enough for him to see how far up was pure skin and how far he might find the proof that she was lying.

Surely she was lying. This was Jane, after all.

"This isn't funny, Jane," he said, feeling hot and dizzy all of a sudden, seeing nothing but her, her legs and that gloriously sexy hot-pink skirt.

"I'm not trying to be funny. I was ready for our date. I was really excited about our date, and right before I left your office yesterday, you said to wear one of my suits without any—"

"Good God, I never thought you'd actually do it!" he yelled.

Passengers in the rows in front of them turned to stare. The first-class flight attendant, who'd been openly flirting with Wyatt as they got on the plane, despite the fact that he was traveling with Jane, now shot him a worried look, as if he might be trouble on this flight.

Jane leaned into him. "I wanted to surprise you."

"Well, you certainly did," he said, none too quietly.

"I thought you'd like it," she said, pouting a bit.

"Like it?" He laughed, sounding as if he was being strangled, all the blood leaving his head and heading south, leaving him decidedly uncomfortable. He shifted in his seat. No help there.

Did she have any idea what she was doing to him?

"I was trying to be…you know…non-prudish," she explained.

"Well, you succeeded."

"I thought you'd be happy—" she repeated.

"Jane, I'd love it, if only I could do something about it," he told her. "But it's a four-hour flight! You're telling me I have four hours to sit here next to you, knowing you're completely bare under that tiny hot-pink skirt and not do anything about it?"

"Oh," she said. "Well, I didn't mean to end up this way on the plane. It was just, with all the commotion over Gram and Gladdy being missing and finding out they'd both eloped with your uncle, I wasn't really thinking about my underwear or lack of it. Until right now."

Wyatt buried his face in his hand, then opened his eyes and stared at her legs again. Couldn't help it.

Jane had really nice legs, toned and lightly tanned.

He looked around at exactly where they were on the plane. It was small. In each row, there were two first-class seats on either side of a single aisle. No one was in the seats directly across from them, and the wall of the first-class cabin was behind them. There were two people in the row in front of them, on the opposite side of the aisle, and Wyatt had taken the aisle seat. If he angled his body the right way…

"What are you doing?" Jane asked suspiciously.

"Just taking stock of the situation we're in, of the options…."

"Options?" She looked aghast. "I want you to know right now that I am not doing anything with you in the lavatory of this airplane. So you can forget that—"

"I didn't ask you to. I wouldn't. I have trouble believing it's even possible myself. I can hardly get my whole body into one of those things, as small as they are these days, although I know people who swear it can be done. Still, it's just not my thing, to do it in an ultra-cramped airplane bathroom. Of course, I've never been on a plane for four hours with a woman with no panties on before."

"You sound so mad at me—"

"Jane, I think I'm going to lose my mind before we ever get off this plane. I'm starting to sweat, and we haven't even taken off yet. Because all I can think about is you…sitting there…and how much I want my hand under your skirt."

She pressed her thighs together as if he'd have a fight on his hands if he tried that.

"I know. Believe me, I know."

"Surely you're capable of showing some kind of restraint. You're a grown man, Wyatt—"

"Do you have any idea how many times I've undressed you in my head?"

She fell silent, looking a bit scared of him, as if he might turn into a raving, sexual beast at any moment and devour her.

"Yeah," he said. Maybe she was beginning to understand the problem now. "I've done it slowly. I've done it in seconds flat. I've taken suits of every color off you, un-buttoned crisp, prim, white blouses with excruciating attention to detail to every bit of skin I uncover. I've ripped buttons away with my teeth, Jane!"

She eased away from him, as far as the side of the airplane would allow, and just stared up at him with wary eyes. "Men don't do those kinds of things to me."

"This man is going to."

"Not here!" she whispered urgently.

"Four hours," he replied. "It's a four-hour flight. I really don't think you understand the urgency of my situation."

"How spoiled are you? You can't wait four hours for a woman?"

Wyatt saw that she still just didn't get it. Did that mean she hadn't even thought of him undressing her seventeen different ways, including with his teeth? Was she completely oblivious to him and this crazy attraction he felt for her?

Maybe all the Gray men had gone crazy at the same time.

Wyatt had an idea.

Jane watched him warily as an odd sense of calm came over him and he stopped arguing with her. His sudden silence, his seeming acceptance of the situation, made her all the more uneasy. But he just sat there, like a man perfectly at ease, big and gorgeous and sexy, taking up way more room than he should have in the seat beside her. He sat there as the plane took off and climbed into the air, wordlessly downing two bourbons during the beverage service, sat there as the captain dimmed the lights and people quieted down and settled in to get some sleep.

Which made Jane feel a little uneasy.

It was darker than she thought it should be, more private here in the last row of the first-class cabin, the curtains behind them drawn shut, the flight attendants settled in, too, up front, no one in the seats immediately to their left.

She clicked on her overhead light.

Wyatt laughed softly, reached across her and clicked it off.

Jane put her hands up to ward him off, but he didn't do anything else, just sat back in his seat, waiting.

For what?

Nervously, she scanned the cabin again, finding it even quieter now, soft voices heard here and there, but muffled, more like the impression of sound than sound itself, the hiss of the plane's ventilation system leaving a kind of white noise around them that enveloped them in a kind of privacy.

So, it was dark and quiet.

That was bad, Jane feared. Very bad.

The truth was, she had put this suit on thinking about him looking at her in it, looking at her as if he was going to devour her whole, which is exactly how he'd looked at her when he found out the secret to this outfit. She'd had vague thoughts about him undressing her very slowly, very carefully, almost politely, although she had known even then that the polite part was definitely more her fantasy than anything he'd ever come up with. And she'd been right about that. He had fantasized about ripping off buttons with his teeth, after all.

So Jane sat there, huddled into her corner, watching him, getting all warm and sleepy and wondering if, given his mood earlier, using him as a big comfy pillow on the way to Vegas was out of the question. She found herself nodding off a bit, her head sinking down to the side of the plane, then jerking awake again.

He stood up, got an airline pillow and blanket out of the overhead bin, then sat back down beside her. He pushed the armrest between them up and out of the way, then put the pillow against his side. His arm around her, he invited her to make herself comfortable against him.

She turned her body toward the window, away from him, bent her legs and tucked them half under her on the seat, then leaned back into him, her head on his shoulder. He might nibble on her ear, if he wanted, but she felt fairly safe in this position.

He didn't object at all, merely spread the blanket over her, as she murmured, "Thank you."

Just drifting off to sleep, she felt his hand, under that blanket, palming her leg at the knee and then slowly sliding up her thigh.

Her eyes flew open and locked on his. She felt in an instant that he'd angled his body toward the window. She glanced anxiously toward the aisle and found her view blocked completely by his shoulder. No doubt, his body was now blocking anyone's view of her.

Which was bad.

Very bad.

And in that time she'd nearly fallen asleep, she'd somehow ended up with her back pressed against the front of his body, her bottom tucked firmly against his lap, and he obviously liked it there, because he was thoroughly aroused.

It was a completely involuntary reaction, she reasoned, as she rubbed her hips against him, and it just felt so very good, she had to do it again. She couldn't help it.

He swore softly and started nibbling on her neck, making her squirm all the more, sensations shooting through her body. That hand of his, beneath the blanket he'd so thoughtfully spread over her, sliding even higher on her thigh. His other hand undid the two buttons on her jacket, then settled warm against her belly, eventually sliding up toward her breasts.

He took his nose and nudged her jacket down her shoulder a bit, used his teeth to pull the tiny strap of her camisole aside, and the next thing she knew, his warm mouth settled on her neck, dropping little kisses up and down the line of her neck and shoulder.

She sucked in a breath, his hands all over her, his mouth too, her body tucked firmly against his and turning liquid in his arms.

"Wyatt, we're on a plane," she protested.

"I know."

"And you said you really weren't into doing things like this in public places."

"I said I wasn't into actually having sex in public places. But since you got on this plane that way, I've decided that's not really a firm conviction of mine."

Before she could object, his hand settled, palm flat, against the curve of her hip.

Her breasts got all tingly and full, her nipples bunching up to knots. His hand finally palmed one of her breasts, as well, his thumb rubbing back and forth on one of her nipples.

His hand felt so big and so hot against her, and the camisole was so thin, it was practically nonexistent. His hands were everywhere. So was his mouth.

"Someone will hear us," she protested.

"Only if you get too loud," he claimed. "I didn't take you for a screamer, Jane. Although I'd certainly like to make you scream. Just not here. Not now. Later, okay?"

"Mmm. Okay. Later."

He kissed her neck some more. Lord, she loved it when he kissed her neck. It just made her melt all over, all hot and shivery and boneless with pleasure. He got his hand under her camisole and back on her breast, skin to skin. She rubbed her bottom against him, feeling a pulse throbbing in him, an answering one in her own body.

Could they really have sex on the plane? Would it be that bad? That dangerous? She could shove a pillow in her mouth and just try very hard to move as little as possible, couldn't she?

She wanted to turn around, wanted so badly to touch him, to feel his skin beneath her hands, but he held her fast. She reached back with one hand and held his head down to her shoulder, and with the other, covered his hand on her breast, urging him not to stop tormenting her this way.

Wyatt touching her, kissing her. It felt so good. He was going to drive her crazy. She knew it. But just how far was he going to take this?

"Wyatt?" she whispered urgently. "What are you going to do to me?"

"This," he said, his mouth against her ear, nibbling there as the hand on her hip slid into the curls between her thighs.

She shook her head. "No. You can't. Not here."

"Why not?" he asked.

"Because…you can't."

But even as she said it, her traitorous body had made room for him there, easing her thighs ever so slightly apart. She shuddered as his fingers moved knowingly into the hot wetness of her body, and his thumb…oh, that thumb.

If he hadn't covered her mouth with his, no telling what kind of noise she would have made then. But he'd anticipated that, silencing her with a long, deep, slow kiss, his touch between her legs just as maddeningly slow and sure.

He thrust inside of her with his tongue, with his fingers, and it took nothing and no time, it seemed before she shuddered against him, having to bite down on her lip to keep from crying out in pleasure, the kind of deep, uncontrollable feelings she hadn't been sure she was capable of feeling.

There was no control at all on her part, nothing she was capable of or willing to do to stop this, to hold it back, to contain it in any way. He was completely in charge. She'd given herself fully into his hands, and he was obviously a master at this. Oddly, she felt both out of control and completely safe in his arms, felt no need to protect herself, to maintain any kind of distance. She was his. She might as well have stripped off all her clothes and presented herself to him naked as could be and invited him to do whatever he wanted. She'd given herself to him that completely. Something she'd never felt safe doing with any man, especially one who looked like him, who had the confidence and obvious experience with women that he did.

Jane lay there in his arms, exhausted, spent, gloriously happy. She couldn't believe it. She just couldn't fathom what he'd done to her and how glorious it had felt, how she couldn't wait to do it again, to do anything he wanted, whenever he wanted.

"This is why women make fools of themselves over men," she told him softly, once she could actually think again and form words.

He laughed, the sound so sexy, and thrust gently against her hips once, then again. "You begin to understand how I felt when you told me you weren't wearing any underwear?"

She nodded, then got it. "Payback? This was payback?"

"No, Jane. This is a little thing called foreplay. What do you think?"

"That if the real thing feels any better, I may die."

"And just think, we only have another three hours before we can get off this plane, find a hotel room and get naked," he told her.

Three hours?

She whimpered. "What are we going to do for three hours?"

"Exactly what we've been doing," he promised.

"No. I can't. We can't. Someone will see us. Someone will hear us. Wyatt!"

But he was kissing her again, and she wanted so much for him to kiss her.

She wanted him to do all sorts of things to her, right here on this plane. He couldn't do much more than he already had, could he? She feared she was about to find out.

Chapter Eleven

She felt as if she'd been drugged by the time they landed in Vegas, as if her entire body was utterly exhausted, limp with the aftermath of foreplay like none she'd ever known before and the added fear of trying to stay quiet enough that the whole plane didn't know what they were doing.

Her skirt was all rumpled and up around her waist under the blanket, her legs like jelly. She had no idea where her shoes had gone. Her hair had either all come loose or Wyatt had taken it down, and she wondered if the stubble on his jaw had left faint reddish marks on her neck and her face.

Not that she really cared, as long as he was kissing her.

But they did have to get off this plane somehow, and she might as well be wearing a giant, blinking sign that said, *Nearly had sex on the plane to Vegas.*

"I feel like such a bad girl," she whispered to him, as

she looked out the window, seeing a sea of neon lights below.

He leaned in beside her, looking out the window himself. "You were a deliciously bad girl on this plane, and now, look at all those hotel rooms below us, all those places for you to be bad, Jane."

She grinned. "Are we going to be bad first, or are we going to hunt down our crazy relatives?"

"Well, it is about 4:00 a.m. our time. Surely they've already done whatever it is they wanted to do and are asleep by now. I figure we have some time before they wake up, so what would it hurt to be bad until the sun comes up?"

He dropped a kiss on her shoulder as he said it, and she wondered just how bad Wyatt, in the privacy of his own room, behind a locked door, could be. She didn't want to disappoint him, although in truth, he seemed delighted in anything she was willing to offer him, so far.

The lights in the cabin came up and the pilot announced that they would be landing soon.

Jane groaned and hid her face against Wyatt, afraid that people had to be staring at them. His body was warm and welcoming, his arm around her, hand on the back of her head, holding her against him. He was chuckling softly.

"How terrible is it?" she asked. "Is everyone watching?"

"Jane, they're all still half-asleep. No one really cares."

She peeked out to the side, seeing no one, and then cautiously looked forward.

"See? It's fine."

"I'm all mussed up," she said.

"Yes, you are." He sounded quite pleased by it.

She brushed her hair back with her fingers and then

faced him, embarrassed as could be without the cover of darkness between them. "You have no shame, do you?"

"Not at the moment." He took her chin in his hand. "And you look absolutely gorgeous like this. Someone should always be mussing you up."

He kissed her softly on the lips, and something in her heart turned over, as if she'd gone to the dark side, too, and never wanted to lose this feeling. She wrapped her arms around him and gave him a big, long, deep kiss in the light, just because. He groaned, took her hips in his palms and pulled her onto his lap. She fell back against him, forgetting everything, until a woman cleared her throat somewhere near Jane's ear.

They came up for air to find the stewardess, the gorgeous one who'd been eyeing Wyatt from the moment he stepped onboard, asking them to buckle their seat belts, because the plane would be landing soon.

And she gave Jane a look that said, *What in the world is he doing with someone like you?*

Jane wanted to shoot right back, *Seeing how bad he can make me,* but shook her head and laughed instead.

Once they landed, Wyatt helped her straighten herself up as best he could and guided her off the plane with a hand riding low on her waist, just enough to feel a little devilish. They grabbed the first cab they found and he asked the driver to take them to the Pallazzo.

"Leo's current favorite, I believe," Wyatt said.

Jane leaned back against him, torn between snuggling in the cab and reaching into her briefcase and turning on her phone to see if Gram or Gladdy had answered any of the frantic messages she left for them or if maybe Lainie had tracked them down while Jane and Wyatt were on the plane.

"Don't do it," Wyatt declared. "If you turn on that phone and have a message from them, it might be hours before we sort out their troubles and can be alone."

"I know," she said, but the ultra-responsible, good-girl tendencies were harder to deny now that they were on the ground in the same city as her sweet but maddening grandmother and great aunt.

"We'll be good and responsible when the sun comes up. I promise."

"Okay, but you might have to take my phone away from me and hide it." She pushed her briefcase over to him. "Here. Really. Just find it and take it."

He fished through her briefcase, came up with the phone and slipped it into his pocket. Then he frowned and said, "It's on. You turned it on when I wasn't looking?"

"No," she insisted. "What do you mean, it's on?"

"I mean, it's vibrating, so it must be on."

"I didn't. I swear." She grabbed the phone out of his pocket and saw that it was indeed on, and she had a call coming in. "I must have forgotten to turn it off when we got on the plane, just left it on vibrate."

"Don't answer it, Jane. If you do, I swear, when I finally get you alone, I will make you pay for making me wait even longer."

Responsibility warred with her overwhelming need for him but responsibility won.

"I'm sorry. Really, I am," she said, answering the incoming call. "Hello."

"Jane! Oh, thank God." It was Lainie.

"Did you find them?" Jane asked.

"No, Gladdy called for you here, when you weren't answering your phone."

"Please tell me they didn't get married already?"

"No. They…actually, I don't know. Jane, they're at the hospital. It… I'm sorry. It sounds bad."

Jane froze, the words just not making any sense at first. "Gram?"

"No, Leo."

Lainie told Jane the name of the hospital and insisted she had no other details, though she'd been trying and trying to call the hospital, Gram and Gladdy, with no response. Stunned, Jane thanked her and clicked off the phone.

"What is it?" Wyatt asked.

Jane slipped her hand into his and held on tight, then gave the cab driver the name of the hospital and asked him to take them there.

Wyatt just looked at her, and she could see him trying to make sense of this in his own head. Leo Gray seemed indestructible to her, and she'd only known him a few weeks. How much more invincible he must have seemed to Wyatt.

"All Lainie knew was that they took Leo to the hospital."

Wyatt still didn't move.

"Has he been ill?" Jane asked softly.

"No. Not that I knew. He's always been incredibly healthy."

He grasped her hand like a lifeline, with his other hand pulled out his own phone, went to click it on, but fumbled it, dropping it instead. Jane went to pick it up for him, but he held up a hand to show that he didn't want it. And his hand was shaking.

"How far to the hospital?" she asked.

"Five minutes, tops," the driver responded.

"Okay," she said to Wyatt, still holding his hand, wishing she could somehow protect him from what could come. "Lainie said neither Gram nor Gladdy are answering their phones anyway. We'll find out how he is in a few minutes."

Wyatt knew the doctor was talking to him. Something about a stroke, Leo unconscious since he'd been brought in and on life support. There were questions about Leo's medical history, his doctors' names. Wyatt had that information. Jane handed over his cell phone, and he found the names and numbers. Did Leo have a living will? Did anyone have power of attorney to act on his behalf if he was incapacitated?

"Yes. I do." A power he'd hoped to never exercise.

The papers? They needed the papers. No, Wyatt didn't walk around with Leo's legal papers on him.

Jane stepped in. Jane still by his side, still firmly holding his hand, saying she'd make the calls, get all the papers, so Wyatt wouldn't have to do anything but see Leo.

Wyatt kissed her forehead, said, "Thank you," and then let a nurse lead him through those ominous-looking double doors into the medical nightmare of machines and cubicles and terrified-looking relatives.

Jane's grandmother was seated by Leo's side, holding his hand and crying softly. She looked absolutely heartbroken, and on her left hand—the one holding Leo's—something caught the light with a flash. A big new diamond ring Wyatt didn't remember seeing before.

Wife number five, Wyatt thought, then remembered that Leo had always held out hope that one day he'd be able to say, "Till death do us part," and mean it.

Wyatt feared his uncle was about to get his wish.

He walked to Kathleen's side, took the hand she offered and then helped her to her feet. She threw her arms around him and wept softly, as Gladdy had done outside in the ICU waiting room.

Women, crazy about Leo and fighting over him to the end, Wyatt thought. How perfectly Leo-like. He sincerely hoped the old man hadn't actually married both women. Settling the estate would be a nightmare if Leo had.

"He was so happy," Kathleen said, still crying. "So very happy. We had a grand time, these last few weeks. Some of the best times of his life, he said. I'm grateful for every moment we had together."

Wyatt smiled, despite feeling as if his heart was breaking.

It was exactly what Leo would have wanted. All it was lacking was Kathleen vowing that he'd been the absolute love of her life and that she'd go to her grave remembering the times she spent with Leo Gray. Her and Gladdy both would have been even better, from Leo's perspective.

"He wanted me to tell you," Kathleen said, "that you were the perfect son to him, all the joy and love without all the responsibility that comes with actually being a parent."

Wyatt laughed, despite himself. "He actually put in more time raising me than my father did."

Leo had never had children of his own, although between them, his four wives had given him a dozen or so stepchildren and unknown hordes of grandchildren, almost all of whom adored Leo and still kept in touch with him.

"I'll leave you two alone." Kathleen hugged him once more, kissed his cheek sweetly, then Leo's. "We'll be right outside if you need us."

* * *

By the time they reached Leo's doctor, they knew everything.

Leo had known for weeks that he had an inoperable condition that could cause a stroke, but for reasons Wyatt could not understand, had decided not to tell anyone. He'd just gone about his life, as it had always been until something like this happened. His best hope was to die with a smile on his face in the arms of a beautiful woman, the doctor remembered Leo saying. Wyatt told him that Leo might very well have gotten his wish.

Bleary-eyed and beyond exhaustion two hours later, he walked out of the ICU and found Jane there waiting for him.

She got to her feet, took his hand in her tiny one, and he wondered at how a man could feel instantly better just holding Jane's hand. She stood up on her tiptoes and kissed Wyatt's cheek. He thought there was nothing he wanted more in this world than to collapse into her arms and have her lie to him and tell him everything was going to be fine, when he knew damn well it wasn't. That things would never be the same again.

Leo had been one of the few constants in Wyatt's mixed-up life, one person he'd always counted on and somehow thought he'd always have. Silly given the fact that the man was eighty-six, but he certainly had seemed as if he would live forever.

"The doctors just have to see the power of attorney from my office," he began, "wait a few more hours and repeat the brain scan, and then…"

"I know," Jane said. "The doctor told Gram everything, given the fact that she has a big, new diamond on her finger and claims to have married Leo sometime last night."

Wyatt nodded. "Please tell me he didn't marry Gladdy, too?"

"No, although he bought her a lovely diamond necklace. A consolation prize? A kind of reverse wedding gift? I don't have any idea. But Gram wanted you and I to know that she and Leo did sign some kind of prenup, because they both had promised us they wouldn't marry again without one. So, they were thinking of us. She said they hoped we wouldn't be too mad at them."

Wyatt shook his head, thought about laughing, then felt his eyes flood with uncharacteristic tears. He wouldn't have to worry any more about Leo and his various wives, his love life, his marriages or him getting kicked out of retirement villages.

"Come on," Jane indicated. "The doctor said it's going to be at least noon before they have everything in order and can…"

"Turn off the machines?"

Jane nodded.

"It's what he wanted," Wyatt told her. "What I promised him I'd do if he ever ended up like this."

"Well, you don't have to do any of it right now. There's a hotel across the street. I had Gram and Gladdy get us all rooms there, and you're going to get some sleep—"

"I can't stand to leave him all alone, Jane."

"Gram's coming to sit with him. She or Gladdy will be with him until you get back. There will be dozens of things you have to take care of in the next few days. Take some time to sleep now, while you can."

"I have to find my father and call him," Wyatt argued.

"I left a voice mail for Lucy at your office. She'll get to

work on finding him as soon as she gets in. Leo has four ex-wives somewhere that we'll need to notify?"

Wyatt nodded. "I don't even know if we can find them all."

"Between Lucy, Lainie and I, we can find anyone. But right now, you're going to sleep."

Wyatt did something he never really did. He put himself into Jane's capable hands and let her take care of him and everything else.

She walked him across the street, met her grandmother in the lobby and got key-cards for their rooms, then took him upstairs into a small suite on the fifteenth floor where the darkened sky outside the massive windows told him it was indeed still nighttime somehow and the glow of neon told him he could only be in Vegas.

There was a room service platter of fruit and cheese waiting for them, which he nibbled on while he grabbed a tiny bottle of bourbon from the minibar. Jane pointed out a fresh suit and tie, plus a few other items of clothing from one of the shops downstairs, were hanging in the closet. Gram used to sell men's suits and could tell just by looking that he was indeed a 42 Long. They had stocked the bathroom with toiletries, and anything else he needed, they would find.

"The Carlton women have been busy," he said.

"Yes, we have. Now sit down and eat something. I'm going to take a quick shower. I don't think I'll be able to sleep feeling this grimy."

He sat down with his drink and nibbled on some fruit, feeling curiously empty inside and mostly just…numb. He may have even dozed a bit in his chair, because the next thing he knew, the whole room smelled wonderful and

Jane was standing in front of him in a pretty, flowery silk robe and a nightgown underneath it, her skin a rosy pink, hair down and damp, just brushing her shoulders.

"I must be dreaming," he said at the sight of her.

"Gram and Gladdy shopped for me, too. I'm sure they figured, What's a little tragedy when Jane might still be able to pick up a man out of the deal? And they so seldom have a chance to dress me as they please. I'm afraid to even see what they expect me to wear tomorrow."

Wyatt grinned, despite his exhaustion. Oddly, he felt as if she was the only thing holding him together right now.

She came to stand behind his chair, leaned over the back of it and put her arms around him, kissing the side of his forehead. He turned his face into her shoulder, to her soft, sweet-smelling skin and her welcoming arms. What a kindhearted, comforting woman.

"Was it really just a few hours ago that we were on the plane, driving each other crazy?"

"Yes," she whispered.

"I want to go back there. Isn't it odd, how you can be somewhere, with someone, and be completely happy, and then… Boom, everything just blows up? And you think, I want to go back. I just want to be there again."

"Wyatt, you're exhausted," she whispered. "Come to bed."

"With you?"

"Yes. We'll just sleep. I'm not leaving you alone tonight."

Which implied that he needed her, and he had to admit to himself at least that in this moment, he did. He did not want to be alone. He didn't want to do so much as let go of her hand after they walked into the suite a moment ago. And yet, he had no idea what to say to her decision that they'd be sharing a bed tonight.

She took his hand and led him into the bedroom, pulled the curtains shut tight, flipped off the lights and turned down the bed. He shrugged out of his jacket, loosened his tie. She started unbuttoning his shirt. He put his hands on hers to stop her, feeling he was drowning or choking all of a sudden, as if all he wanted to do was fall into her arms and beg her to never let him go, something the Gray men certainly didn't do.

"I'm going to grab a shower, too," he said, mostly because if he actually did fall apart, he certainly didn't want to do it in front of her. So he slid that pretty robe off her shoulders and tucked her into bed. "Go to sleep. I'll be here in a few minutes."

And then he fled into the bathroom, got rid of the tie, the shirt, splashed water on his face and then leaned over the sink, propped up on his hands and stared at his own reflection in the big mirror. His eyes were heading toward bloodshot. He needed a shave. His hands were shaking again, and he still felt as if he was drowning.

The shower didn't really help, although it felt better to be clean. He dried off, wrapped a towel around his waist, brushed his teeth, even shaved, because he'd already scuffed up Jane's pretty, delicate skin with what he'd done to her on the plane, and if he got anywhere near her in that bed, he'd rough her up even more.

He walked into the bedroom, saw her sleeping quietly on her side. Would he still feel as if he was choking if he climbed into bed with her and pulled her against him? Or would that just make things worse? Make him want her? Want her to help him forget, just for a few moments? None of which was fair to her at all, and besides, he didn't use women that way. He didn't ask them to comfort him or make him forget anything.

But he hadn't asked her to do any of the things she had tonight. She'd just done them, just like she was waiting there in the bed for him, Jane all soft and sweet-smelling and even soothing, as amazing as that was.

He looked down to see that her eyes were open, barely.

"Wyatt, come to bed." She pulled back the covers, and rolled over on the mattress to face the far side of the bed, making room for him.

He dropped the towel around his waist and got into bed. Rolling onto his side, he fit the front of his body to the back of hers, tucking her fully against him ever so carefully, as if she was made of something so fragile she might break.

He'd intended to take good care of her, and arrogant as it was, he knew he could show her things in bed that no other man ever had, taking her places she'd never been before. Somehow, no one had ever taken the time or cared enough to truly please her. It was so obvious from the surprise and sheer delight she'd shown at the least little things he'd done to her on the plane. How she could be that innocent in this day and age, he didn't understand, but he intended to be the one who showed her all the pleasures there could be between a man and a woman. And this certainly wasn't the time or the place for any of it.

Closing his eyes, he knew that.

His body, exhausted as it was, just hadn't quite figured it out yet. Having her cute little fanny pressed up against his groin wasn't helping, either.

He groaned softly but couldn't bring himself to move away. It wouldn't be the first night he'd spent wanting Jane, but it would be the first he'd had to spend in the same bed with her, wanting her but not doing anything about it.

He willed himself to relax, to breathe deeply and evenly, not to thrust ever so gently against the curve of her bottom.

She laughed softly, sleepily, rolled over and looked up at him through the darkness of the night. "Let me guess. Gram and Gladdy left you with nothing to wear to bed?"

"Well, you said that to them, everything's an opportunity to further your love life."

She nodded, placed her palms against his bare chest, running them softly over his skin. He'd been aching for her to touch him this way, to feel those small, soft hands all over his body. It was going to kill him to push her away.

He put his hands on her wrists. "Jane, this is not what I wanted for us. Not at all what I intended."

"I know," she agreed. "But I think it's what you need, and it's what I want to give you."

She pulled her hands free, rolled away from him ever so slightly and then took her nightgown, pulled it up over her head and tossed it onto the floor.

Chapter Twelve

He was too stunned to say anything or to do anything, either.

Jane? Sweet, shy, prim and proper Jane? Peeling off her nightgown, just like that?

When she rolled back into his arms, they were skin to skin, those soft breasts he'd teased mercilessly on the plane nestled against his bare chest, his erection surging against her belly.

She wrapped her arms around him and kissed him softly, gently, and he let her, too shocked to do anything else. He'd always been a man in control in bed, a generous, thoughtful lover, he would have said. He tried to make sure he always gave much more than he ever took.

And here he was with Jane—this was Jane in his bed—shaking like an inexperienced boy, feeling as if he had the same lack of control as one, and yet still wanting to take care of her, to give her more than he'd ever given any woman.

It didn't make any sense. Nothing did tonight.

She kept right on kissing him, her mouth a sweet, shy temptation, her body warm and supple against his. He took control of the kiss, devouring her, grabbing her and crushing her to him with no finesse at all, feeling raw inside and out. That choking feeling was still there, that sensation that nothing in the world made sense, and she was his only lifeline, his only hope.

He kissed her lovely, highly responsive neck, sucked hard on her nipple, slipped a hand between her legs and nearly went insane when he felt how soft and wet and ready she was.

There had to be more, he told himself, something better for her, something to make her want him back in her bed over and over again, but he just couldn't think what that might be. All he could think about was getting inside her, being a part of her, having that connection, at least for a little while.

He went to push her away, to buy himself a moment to think, to take some time with her and show her that she was so very special to him, that she was different. But she only let him push her away long enough to roll onto her back, let her thighs fall open and pull him on top of her.

He didn't so much as take a breath before he was slipping inside of her. And she welcomed him. She had her hands on his hips, pulling him to her, her body rising up to meet his, as if he was the only thing she wanted in this world. It was so easy and felt so good and seemed like everything he needed in that moment. She felt so small beneath him. He was sure he would crush her, and yet, she didn't seem to care. He eased in a bit more, let his forehead fall down to hers.

"Jane," he said, kissing her urgently.

She wrapped her legs around his waist and he sank inside her all the way, her body gripping his in a hot, sweet hold that had him gritting his teeth and ready to beg her to be still, just for a moment. But she showed no mercy, rocking her body against his, her nails sinking into his hips.

Sweet, generous Jane. Taking him.

He lost all control, cried out, rocked hard against her again and again. There was no stopping it. There was nothing. Just her, accepting, urging him on, giving, and him done, just like that, in an instant, a hot, mind-blowing surge of ecstasy and regret.

Once he was capable of the most basic thought, he swore softly at what he'd done. He wasn't even wearing a condom. Sixteen years of scrupulously safe sex, and he didn't even have a damn condom on tonight. With her.

And that choking feeling was back.

As if she'd ripped open wounds deep inside that might never heal, feelings he'd never be able to stuff back inside him.

"It's all right," she told him, kissing his cheek, holding him tightly against her, her body throbbing against his. "Everything's all right."

He didn't even know if he'd managed to bring her to satisfaction, but he doubted it, couldn't remember anything except that exquisite feeling of release, of every thought draining from his head except for how good it felt to be right there inside her, and that it was Jane, and the way she'd just brought him into her, welcomed him, like a man coming home from a long, difficult, lonely journey in the dark.

And what had he done for her? Next to nothing, he feared. *Dammit.* What in the hell was wrong with him?

He had his head buried against her neck, lying heavily on top of her and feeling too exhausted to move an inch, and he thought there were tears seeping out of the corners of his eyes.

She had tears, too. He felt them rolling slowly down her cheek.

He managed to lift his head, look down into her glistening eyes. She gave him a sad smile, her hands on his cheek, kissed him sweetly one last time and when he went to say something, anything, pressed her fingers to his lips.

"Go to sleep, Wyatt. Just sleep."

He rolled off her and onto his back, having no idea what to think, what to do. She rolled into his side, draping one leg over his, laid her head against his chest, one hand over his heart.

Regret, bone-deep satisfaction and need warred within him, only to be edged out by complete exhaustion and the kind of all-over relaxation that only came from a night spent with a woman.

Or maybe it was a night spent with Jane, giving herself so sweetly to him and asking for nothing in return. An ease, a sense of peace came over him as he let the feel of her curled up against him fill all the empty spaces inside of him.

He wanted her, still. It was like a low hum of sexual need that he wasn't sure would ever go away, but there was something else, too. Something new and different, completely baffling.

He wanted to just be here with her, hold her, just know she was here, and that he wasn't alone. That choking feeling was easing. It felt as if every muscle in his body relaxed as she lay in his arms and the world finally faded to black.

* * *

He woke from a dead sleep, with no idea what time it was, where he was or how he'd gotten there at first, and then it all came rushing back.

A hotel. Vegas. Leo. Jane.

He rolled over and could still smell her sweet scent on the pillow beside him. He was alone in the bed at… He glanced at the clock. Both hands on the twelve. Noon? Looking at the closed curtains, he saw light bleeding through the edges.

Yes, noon. Not midnight, though he could have slept round the clock. He felt as if he was hung over, his limbs nearly too heavy to move, flashes of the night before moving slowly through his muddled brain.

Leo was dying. They were going to pull the plug today. Wyatt had to sign the papers to let him go.

And Jane…Jane was…taking care of him? Was that how she saw it? Sweet, innocent, giving Jane.

He remembered so clearly the feel of her body beneath his, of her taking him inside her and tears running down her cheeks and his when they were done. The feel of her soft hands and gentle heart, her pretty breasts and the temptation of her mouth.

He swore once again, wishing there was some way to take back what had happened and thinking of how he could make it up to her, and then remembering the condom part.

The no-condom part.

Good God, how could he be so irresponsible?

It was as if he'd woken up and didn't even recognize himself and the way he'd behaved in the dark hours of the night.

He threw back the covers and walked into the shower, hoping the water would help wake him up. Dressing quickly in the suit he found in the closet, he took a few moments to brace himself for facing whomever was on the other side of that door and whatever might have happened in the hours he'd been asleep, and then walked into the living room of the suite.

Jane was there, dressed in a pretty, flowery, silky dress that showed off all her curves, cut high on the thigh and scooped out low on the neckline.

Kathleen and Gladdy's work, no doubt.

She was sitting at the desk, talking on her cell phone, a pad of paper in front of her, pen in hand, taking notes.

She smiled welcomingly when she saw him and pointed to a pot of coffee and some food on a room service cart by the window. He took the coffee and gulped it down, because his brain still felt muddled and slow.

He had no idea what to say to her, how to make up for what he'd done or to thank her for all the things she and her relatives had taken care of last night.

All too soon, before the coffee had done its work, she was off the phone and stood up, list in hand. Coming to him, she put her hand on his arm and got up on her tiptoes to kiss him softly on the cheek.

"Sleep well?" she asked.

"Like the dead," he said, then stopped, realizing what he'd said. *Damn. Leo.* "He's not gone yet, is he?"

"No. Gladdy just called. The doctors have all the paperwork they need on the health care power of attorney and the living will. They should have the results of the last brain scan in an hour or so. They'll be waiting for you, whenever you're ready."

He shook his head and swore softly.

"I'm sorry," Jane said. "I know people are never really

ready, not with someone as full of life and healthy as…well, as he seemed, as we all thought he was."

"I can't understand why he didn't tell me," Wyatt said.

"Maybe he tried, and he just couldn't. Or maybe he thought it would be easier this way. Maybe he thought there would be time. I mean, we always think there'll be time for the things we want to do or the things we don't always say to the people we love. Don't we?"

Wyatt shook his head, lost. "I just never thought of a world without him. It sounds so stupid to say now. I mean, he's eighty-six, but—"

"I know. I never really thought of a world without Gram or Gladdy, either."

"Jane?" He looked down at her, at how pretty she looked this morning, how sweet, and how capable with her list in hand, things checked off neatly one by one. "Last night… I don't even know what to say."

"There's nothing you need to say," she insisted.

"Yes. There is. There's a ton of things I need to say. For God's sake, I wasn't even wearing a condom. It's…inexcusable, I know."

"Wyatt, I'm sure it won't be a problem. I'm on the pill. And I bet you're normally very responsible about these things—"

"Very," he insisted.

"So, I can't imagine there's any need to worry about any of that."

He let out a long, slow breath. *Okay.* One thing down.

"I'm sorry," he began again. "I would never want to hurt you. Never want to take a chance of hurting you—"

"I know that," she said, as if the thought never even entered her mind.

Good. Okay, now for the rest of it. "I don't normally…" he continued. "I mean, I didn't mean for any of that to happen last night. I was just… I…"

"Wyatt, I know." She held on to his hand and gazed at him, a perfect model of acceptance and reassurance and…

He didn't even know what else he saw in her eyes, but it eased some of the feelings of complete chaos inside him, eased that choking feeling that was back. *Dammit*.

"It wasn't at all what I planned for the first time you and I were together," he tried to explain.

"I know that, too. You don't have anything to apologize for. There's nothing you need to do, except get through this day and try to let me help you do it. Okay?"

He frowned. "I don't…"

"Normally let anyone help you? Or take care of you?" she guessed. "Believe me, that's obvious. Neither do I. So I know just how uncomfortable this would make you, because I would just hate it, hate to ever be in the position where I needed anyone's help. But give it your best shot, okay? It's just one of those…awful times and I'm not letting you do this alone."

"Okay," he said, thinking he couldn't imagine what he'd done to deserve her, but so grateful to have her right now.

"Sit down. Have some more coffee. Try to eat something, and I'll tell you what Lucy and I have done so far."

Jane had accomplished all she could think to do. She'd taken care of Wyatt as best she could, done as much on the phone as possible to get all the legal papers and medical records here, gotten a list of Leo's ex-wives and contact information for all of them. Gladdy remembered where

Leo kept his address book, because she'd been in his room one day when he had sent flowers to one of his ex-wives for her birthday, something he always did for all his exes he had told her. So finding them turned out to be easy.

Lucy said Wyatt hadn't seen his mother in at least a decade and that they shouldn't waste time trying to find her now. His father was somewhere on a remote Greek island, last they'd heard. No one knew if they'd be able to get a message to him before the funeral, which it turned out Leo had already arranged himself. So there was very little to do for that except find the funeral home—that number was in Leo's address book also, which Lainie had gone to Remington Park to retrieve for Jane—and tell them they would soon be putting Leo's plans in place.

And by finishing all that, she hadn't had much time to actually think about spending the night in Wyatt's bed, until she found herself watching him walk into the ICU that day, Gladdy walking out a few moments later, looking a bit frail and sad, two words Jane would never have used before to describe Gladdy or Gram.

Gladdy brightened at the sight of her. She came to sit by Jane in the waiting area, taking Jane's hand in both of hers.

"Darling, that dress is absolutely perfect on you. I knew it would be," she said, then whispered. "And unless I've forgotten what it looks like, I do believe I see a little whisker burn on your neck."

"Gladdy, a man is dying in there!" Jane cried out.

"Yes, darling, he is, but the rest of us aren't, and if anything, losing Leo says to me that we really don't have time to waste here. Anything can happen. At any time. And you've been squandering time for too long, Jane."

Jane was taken aback by that. Gladdy thought she'd been wasting time? Jane would never waste anything as precious as time. The great value she placed on organization alone would ensure that she did not waste time.

"Now sit here and tell me what you and that gorgeous boy of Leo's have been doing, because I could tell the first moment I saw you that you've been up to something with him." Gladdy got a little twinkle in her eyes. "Did he like the nightgown Kathleen and I picked out?"

Jane glared at Gladdy for a moment. She'd still been thinking of time and how she didn't waste it, and here was Gladdy quizzing her about her love life. It just seemed wrong. Wrong, wrong, wrong. To talk like this with Leo soon to take his last breath and not fifty feet away.

"Oh, don't look at me like that. It's what Leo wanted," Gladdy claimed.

"What Leo wanted?"

"You and Wyatt. He was so happy about it."

"How could Leo be happy about it? I thought Leo Gray was insane. I nearly assaulted the man at the retirement park—"

"Oh, he didn't mind that. He said Wyatt needed a woman with fire and spirit inside her."

Jane blinked to clear her vision, thinking she must not have understood. "Leo Gray wanted me to get together with Wyatt?"

"Of course. So you have nothing to feel guilty about. Or… I mean, I'm hoping you did something, but you don't have to feel guilty about it. Now tell me. Right now. We don't know how much time Kathleen and I have to look out for you, Jane. None of us ever really knows. You have to let us help you now while we can."

And then Jane just wanted to cry.

She'd been thinking the very same thing since she had heard about Leo and saw how devastated Wyatt was at the idea of losing him, how shocking it was to him. She felt the exact same way about Gram and Gladdy. She simply could not imagine being without them.

"Tell me," Gladdy prompted. "Tell me the good stuff. I need to hear good things today."

So Jane told her. "Yes, he liked the nightgown, although you could have bought him some pajamas. I mean, that was a pretty obvious omission."

"I'm too old to be subtle. Tell me."

"We…we spent the night together—"

"Jane, please. No subtleties, remember. You made love to that gorgeous man?"

"Yes. He was so sad, and I just…couldn't stand the idea of him being so sad or so alone, so lost, and… I wanted to take care of him. I had to. Have you ever wanted to take care of a man, Gladdy? Felt like you couldn't stand the idea of him being in pain or alone, and that you'd do anything you could to stop him from feeling like that?"

A huge smile spread across Gladdy's face. "Oh, Jane, darling!"

"What?"

"You love him," she whispered.

"No!" Jane insisted. "I didn't say anything about love. I don't want to love any man, and he certainly doesn't want a woman to love him. Not on anything other than a temporary basis. I mean, this is Leo Gray's nephew we're talking about. I bet he's had as many women chasing after him as Leo, and he always will. No sane woman could love a man like that! She'd just be begging to get hurt. I know that."

Gladdy shook her head. "Forget that. Tell me more about wanting to take care of him."

"I just… I had to. Given the situation and…" Jane frowned. A little uneasy feeling in the pit of her stomach that had been there most of the night was steadily getting worse.

"Jane, have you ever wanted to take care of a man before?"

"Well…no," she admitted.

"And I'm betting you've never made love to a man because you were worried about him or in an effort to take care of him?"

"Of course not."

Gladdy just smiled and patted Jane's hand. "So, how was it, dear?"

Jane's cheeks positively burned. Sex, to her, more than anything else, had been an awkward thing, a this-is-what-the-big-fuss-is-about kind of thing. She always felt as if she tried so hard, as if it was work, almost, to try to have what other people claimed to have in bed, and should it really be work-like? In the end—what she'd had—certainly hadn't been anything to write home about, nothing to make her blush so furiously, until now.

Wyatt on the plane had been a revelation, a stunner, an absolute delight, and she'd been nervous about how things would actually go, alone in a bedroom with him. About whether the awkwardness that had always plagued her would return or whether she might disappoint him in any way. Although honestly, when they'd stepped off that plane, she'd been ready and eager to do anything he wanted and to let him do anything he wanted to her.

But what it had been, later, after they found out about Leo, was just…

She couldn't really say what it had been, didn't know exactly how, but it had changed things. Maybe everything. It was nothing about finesse or performance or awkwardness or anything sex had ever been for her before.

She simply had to have him in her arms, inside her, holding nothing back, giving him everything she had to give, him as vulnerable as he could be and her feeling just as vulnerable, but unable to put up the barest hint of defenses against him, against what she was feeling.

Jane had cried softly in his arms afterward, and felt as if there was no place else in the world she'd ever been that was as important as being with him last night.

What in the world did that mean?

She had no idea.

"Wow," Gladdy said. "That good?"

The next twenty-four hours were a blur to Wyatt. He'd prepared himself to sign the release for the hospital to discontinue Leo's life support, but Jane's grandmother stepped in, insisting gently that she, as his wife, be allowed to do it, to spare him, he was sure. The doctors were fine with that, as long as they were all in agreement about what had to be done, and Wyatt surprised himself by letting her sign.

She and Gladdy stood on either side of Wyatt by Leo's bedside as he slipped away quietly and peacefully, and then the Carlton women set to work once more, arranging to have the body flown home with the four of them the next day, arranging for the funeral home in Maryland to be ready to meet their plane when it landed. Jane even called all the ex-wives and listened as one by one, they fell apart and proclaimed their undying devotion and love for Leo.

Soon, Wyatt was back on a plane, this time heading home, Jane once again by his side, her grandmother and Gladdy in the row of seats in front of them. He looked down at the armrest between him and Jane, his arm stretched out along it, Jane's small, soft hand resting in his. There'd hardly been a moment since they'd first heard about Leo that he hadn't had Jane's hand tucked into his.

It was a connection that completely baffled him.

Just a hand, just a touch that meant she was by his side, often not saying anything at all, just being there and taking care of things, so he didn't have to.

And both nights they'd been in Vegas, she'd slept in his bed, in his arms. He'd held her. He'd kissed her. He'd made love to her in an act that spoke more of desperation and need than any he'd ever committed before. He simply hadn't been able to help himself or do any better by her, for her. And what had she done? Opened up her arms and welcomed him into her body, as accepting and kind as a woman could be.

Wyatt was baffled by the whole thing.

All he knew was that he was glad she was there, with him, still holding his hand. That it felt as if she understood, that she hurt when he hurt, and that she cared, that she wouldn't leave him.

But all women left, in the end. No one ever really stayed. Wyatt learned that young. His mother walked out on him and his father when he was six, and his father had remarried not long afterward, to a woman who hadn't really wanted Wyatt around all that much. So he'd gone to live with Leo, but even Leo had left now.

Jane would leave, too.

They were headed back to their real lives. They would

put Leo in the ground, and life would go on. This whole thing, this trip, this time out of time, wasn't real. Wyatt knew that. This thing between him and Jane, unsettling as it was, wasn't real.

She didn't believe a man and woman could build a life together that lasted any more than Wyatt did. It had been one of the first things he'd enjoyed about her—that she understood, that they were in absolute agreement on that point.

And here he was, her hand in his, thinking of how different things had been just forty-eight hours ago, the two of them on another plane, him thinking of nothing else but what he planned to do with her once he got her alone in a bed.

Life was so strange sometimes, he thought.

They'd never gotten that time together, not the way he'd wanted it. He'd wanted to dazzle her, shock her, push her to the very limits she'd allow, and then…of course, eventually, it would all turn out to be like any other relationship he'd ever had. He'd leave her or she'd leave him. That was what was supposed to happen.

Not all this baffling loss and sad, needy sex and him feeling as if she simply belonged here, holding his hand. It was wrong. All wrong. And he had to get things back to the way they were supposed to be, to the life he'd always lived. Normal life, just with Leo gone.

He looked down at Jane, in another of those pretty, flirty, silk-print dresses her relatives had provided for her, that stopped halfway up her thigh and showed off her neck and just a hint of her pretty breasts.

"Nice dress," he said.

"You know who to thank for that."

She smiled, sweetly and sadly at the same time, but he

couldn't have any of that. No more sad. No more her taking care of him. It had to end. Then she put her hand on the side of his face, pulled his mouth down to hers and kissed him, more sweetness and sadness and need there.

How could that be such a potent combination?

Need?

He'd needed women before. Dozens of them. But never like this. He felt that choking sensation again. *Dammit.* When was that going to go away?

Jane shifted in her seat, turning her back to him, then almost to face him. She pushed the armrest between them out of the way, and wrapped her arms around him, snuggling against his chest like a woman with a perfect right to be there. Jane, warm and soft and nearly in the same position she'd slept in the night before, practically on top of him.

He'd stayed awake long into the night, despite being exhausted, and had held her, had stroked a hand through her hair, down her back, across that delicious curve of her hips. He had constantly reassured himself that she was there and loved the sensation of all that bare skin of hers beneath his hands.

"Wyatt?" she whispered, her head tucked beneath his chin. "Let it go."

"Let what go?"

"Everything that's running through your head. Just let it go. Let it be. You don't have to figure anything out right now. There'll be plenty of time for that later."

How did she know, he wondered? It was as if she saw inside him. Saw everything? How had that happened? How could he stop it? How could he shove back down all these feelings?

And then she kissed him again.

There was no heat to it, no fire.

Her kiss said, *I'm sorry. I'm here. Let me make it better now.*

Chapter Thirteen

Wyatt wanted the funeral over with, so they'd scheduled it for one o'clock, the day after they got back from Vegas. They'd left his car at the airport, and Wyatt had driven Kathleen and Gladdy back to Remington Park, then found himself alone with Jane, who'd simply turned to him and asked, "My place or yours?"

He'd hesitated just a beat, then said, "Mine."

That was it. She'd come home with him, been naked in his bed, warm and willing once again, and been up long before him the next morning. He found her wearing what had to be another dress supplied by Kathleen and Gladdy, hair up, pen and pad of paper in hand, looking efficient and hardworking as could be.

Except, she was in his apartment, having made herself at home at least enough to make a pot of coffee and have what looked like the remains of an English muffin and peanut butter. Probably hadn't been much to choose from here, Wyatt knew, thinking it didn't sound half-bad.

He had coffee, put a muffin in the toaster for himself and found the peanut butter. He ate standing in the kitchen, looking at her legs as she finished her phone call, came to kiss him good-morning and tell him she needed to go by her apartment before the funeral to put on her black suit.

Wyatt frowned.

Had he missed something? Was this her taking care of him some more, or had there been some agreement he'd completely forgotten about on her moving in here?

"What's wrong?" she asked.

"Nothing," he claimed.

"I checked with the funeral home. Everything's in order. Still no word from your father—"

"I really didn't expect him to make it, Jane."

"Okay. All four ex-wives are coming."

"Great." Wyatt could just imagine fights breaking out over the seating arrangements among the wives.

"I wouldn't normally mention anything to do with the will right now, but Lucy's afraid you might get questions about it at the service. Apparently, some of the exes are quite anxious about… I guess, Leo had been very generous to them and some of their children over the years—"

Wyatt shook his head and laughed. "Yes, he was a very generous man. I'm sure they're all hoping for the same in his will. Honestly, I can't remember exactly what he did in his most recent will, even though I drew it up for him. He changed it a lot."

"Well, I thought I should warn you, that you might want to dodge them today."

"I have a feeling they will not be delayed on any questions about money. God, they want everything they can get from him, right to the end."

"I could do my best to run interference, once I figure out who's who," she offered.

"You're going to protect me from the money-grubbing ex-wives?" He loved that she wanted to try, but she looked like a pixie next to most adult women.

She frowned. "I can do it. I'm not afraid of anybody. Plus, they take one look at me and expect me to be a pushover, so I have the advantage going in. I'm much tougher than I look."

He wanted to come right back with, *Jane, women do not protect me.* But clearly, she thought she needed to, and it was kind of sweet, once he'd gotten used to the idea and as long as it was temporary. Say, until they got Leo in the ground, he supposed.

And since Jane's particular brand of comfort included her sweet, generous, willing body in his bed, was he really going to object? Even if the whole Jane-moving-in feeling left him…uneasy. Grateful, at the moment, but uneasy.

"Okay, tough girl," he said. "Let's see what you can do against the four of them."

He drove her to her townhouse, not surprised to find it neat, efficient, comfortable and without a single thing out of place. This was definitely Jane.

"A great investment," she told him, as they walked in the door.

"I never doubted it for a second," he said, standing in the living room, looking around while she got dressed in the back bedroom.

The walls were a cheery yellow, the old, hardwood floors gleaming, a brick fireplace dominating the room.

And the whole place smelled like her. He wished he could just stay here all day instead of having to face the funeral.

Jane returned a few minutes later in one of her signature power suits, this time in black, but with what he thought might be another camisole underneath it instead of the usual prim, white blouse. This one was a silky-looking, light grayish-blue thing that left her throat and a bit of her chest bare.

"Stepping out of your comfort zone once again?" he teased, because teasing her sounded like a good idea, like a good thing to help him get through the day.

She was so cute when she was being teased, particularly about her clothing. "I just thought, maybe I've been in a rut lately. You don't think it's inappropriate, do you?"

"Not at all. In fact, women have always looked their best for Leo. I'm thinking we're in for something akin to a fashion show in funeral apparel."

"Really? Maybe I should change."

"No. Trust me. This is perfect."

He'd gotten to her side by then, seen that it was indeed a silk camisole, slipped the jacket off one shoulder and seen the tiny little straps that held the camisole up and all that delicious skin of hers underneath. With the jacket on, she looked perfectly professional and even somewhat modest. Perfect for Jane. But underneath was all that skin, and he'd be the only one who knew.

They drove to Remington Park to pick up Kathleen and Gladdy, who were waiting at the curb for them as they arrived.

"Look at them," Jane said. "They look like they've been at the salon all morning. Their hair just so, their best jewelry on, great shoes. Are those gloves? Wyatt, they're wearing gloves. I'm feeling intimidated by the fashion choices of two eighty-something-year-olds."

"You come from a family of good-looking women, Jane. You're going to be gorgeous when you're eighty."

He got out of the car, kissed each of them on the cheek, telling them they looked fabulous and that Leo definitely would have approved. They beamed up at him as he helped them into the car, then, almost in unison, pulled out white lace hankies and dabbed delicately at the corners of their eyes, the perfect vision of class, high fashion and bereavement.

They arrived at the funeral home to find a mob scene, though they were there a full forty-five minutes early. The funeral director met them at the door. Kathleen stepped up and identified herself as the widow, obviously expecting the great respect due to her, even if she and Leo had only been married for a few hours.

Wyatt wondered how that would go over with the four ex-wives.

The director apologized for the lack of space to accommodate the crowd and promised his staff was opening another room and setting up more chairs as they spoke.

"It appears your husband was an extremely well-known and well-loved man, Mrs. Gray," the director told Gram.

"Oh, he was," she said, she and Gladdy clinging to each other, hankies out and at the ready.

Inside, they walked past a large room overflowing with women, just as Wyatt expected. He saw more of the gloves that had so surprised Jane, more white hankies, a few hats here and there, and an abundance of jewelry, especially diamonds.

Jane stopped in her tracks. "There must be five hundred women in there."

"You expected less?" Wyatt asked.

"And you're right. It looks like a funeral-wear fashion show. Like somebody put out a casting call for over-fifty models. I didn't know there were this many gorgeous women of a certain age in this city."

"The Gray men have always been blessed with a gift for finding attractive women," he said.

Speaking of which, he thought he saw more than one ex-girlfriend of his own in the crowd. Just what he needed today. He eased closer to Jane and put a proprietary hand low on her waist, just a touch above her bottom. She all but melted under his touch, easing into his side as if she belonged there. It just felt so good to have her close.

"Look out. Money-grubbing ex-wives ahead," he said, seeing two of them, maybe even three. It had been a long time since he'd seen Number Three and wasn't absolutely sure he'd recognize her anymore.

"Which ones?" she began, then stopped once again at the sight of them, sitting prominently in the front row in the little room reserved for immediate family. "Fur? They're wearing fur? In May?"

"Fashion faux pas?" he asked.

"I don't know. It just seems a bit much."

Both women got up and approached him, each trying to edge out the other to be the first to reach Wyatt.

He was amused to see that Jane took her protective duties seriously. She planted herself firmly in their path, sticking out a hand and introducing herself, then asking if they'd met Leo's widow.

Faces fell at the word *widow,* concerned looks came out, and both women stood a little straighter, shoulders back, chests out, as if they were getting ready for inspection or as if there might soon be an all-out battle for the former affections of Leo Gray.

Kathleen bore their scrutiny with good grace and a hint of steeliness Wyatt couldn't help but admire, launching into an account of her love and devotion to the man.

"Good move, Jane," Wyatt said admiringly, as she came back to his side and tucked her hand into the crook of his elbow.

"That should stall them for a while. Gram and Gladdy can hold their own against anyone, particularly in things concerning a man."

Another ex-wife walked into the room, obviously recognizing Wyatt and making a beeline for him.

"Number Three," Wyatt warned. "She looks like she might step right over you, if you try to get in her way, Jane. Number Three always was kind of mean."

"This is ridiculous," Jane said, taking Wyatt by the arm and leading him away.

He went willingly, following her down the hall and through a door marked Private that turned out to be a walk-in closet with cleaning supplies and paper products. Jane shut the door behind them, plunging the small, windowless space in total darkness. Wyatt felt her reach for him, her hand landing on his arm, then his chest.

His arms closed around her, fitting her body to his, tucking the back of her head against his shoulder, his other hand wandering down until it rested low on her waist. "Distract me, Jane," he whispered, nuzzling her delicious neck.

"In a funeral home?"

"You could do it," he told her, pressing her up against the wall, telling himself he could kiss her here, just for a minute or two. "Leo wouldn't mind a bit. And I don't see any reason to go back out there just yet."

He endured the funeral, mostly by thinking of those few stolen moments in the closet with Jane, kissing her, his hands wandering, her complaining that he'd left her all mussed up.

Just the way he liked her.

Even with the distraction, it was still nearly too much to fathom, being in the same room for the last time with Leo's body, with all these people who knew and loved him, all these women who wanted him and his money, and then Wyatt imagining a world without him.

He did get a kick out of the pretty women there, just the effort they'd obviously made to look their best for Leo one last time, and the over-the-top, downright theatrical mourning. The place was filled with sobs and delicate tears and hankies.

Wyatt held on to Jane's hand and tried to block out the tributes Leo's friends made to him, to his love of life, his energy, his exuberance, the sheer joy with which he approached each and every day.

Someone had insisted on a reception in Leo's honor afterward at Remington Park, something else which Wyatt endured, keeping Jane close to him, allowing her to act as a buffer between him and the rest of the world.

Thankfully, by early evening, he was once again back in his own apartment, alone with Jane. He hadn't asked if she'd wanted to or planned to come back here with him. He'd just brought her and kept her, because that's what he'd wanted.

And now she was standing there, just inside the door, in her little black suit with the pretty gray-blue camisole, looking up at him as if she was ready once again to give him anything he wanted, anything he might need to get through the day.

What kind of man argued with that?

He'd have to be crazy.

"Jane?" he asked, in a warm, sexy tone that had her heartbeat kicking up a notch as he closed the door behind them once they got into his apartment.

"Yes?" she answered, thinking if he had some sort of distraction in mind, if that's what he needed, she was certainly willing.

He claimed her, that big, glorious body of his crowding her until her back was pressed against the wall, and his body settled against hers. She brought her hands up instinctively, not pushing him away, but resting against his chest, on his shoulders, then winding around his neck.

"Seeing you in that little suit reminds me of you on the plane to Vegas."

She grinned. "I liked our plane ride to Vegas."

"Me too."

As he said it, his hands skimmed over her, inside her jacket, down over the curves of her breasts, his mouth dipping into that spot on her neck that made her just crazy. She felt the heat of him seeping into her body, her blood pounding, her breasts heavy and aching, wanting his attention, his hands, his mouth.

He took his hand and palmed her hips through her clothes, pulling her up and to his body, until she could feel he was aroused, as well, a little thrill shooting through her that she had done this to him. Her. Mousy little Jane. The Queen of Awkward Sex Jane.

She'd never felt the least bit awkward with him.

He took her in a flurry of eagerness and need, hands flying over her, taking the time to do nothing but push her camisole up, so he could get his mouth on her breasts, and pulling off her panties and throwing them on the floor behind him.

His hot hands took her hips and lifted them, lifted her, holding her against the wall with his body as he unzipped his pants and down they went, along with his briefs. He started thrusting, teasingly, against the opening of her body, right there without actually being there, sliding along the mouth of that slick opening, sliding in, just a hint, then gone again.

"Wyatt," she begged.

He didn't tease her, didn't make her wait, not in the three nights they'd spent together. He just came to her, filled her, gave himself to her, all need and raw emotion and blinding pleasure. She hadn't known what to think at first, what to say, what to do, and then realized she didn't have to do a thing, just give herself to him, that it was more than enough.

She clutched at his shoulders, loving the feel of his big, hard body, the sheer bulk of the man. Her thighs fell open even wider, her legs clutching his hips, trying to get him where she wanted him, inside her.

He wouldn't let her.

"What?" she asked. "What are you waiting for?"

"You," he muttered, his mouth against hers, making it clear who was in charge here, who was in control.

She let her nails sink into his back, her other hand into his hair. She whimpered, squirmed against him and that maddening, teasing rhythm he'd set, still not even inside her in that aching, empty space in her body.

He shifted his weight and hers, holding her to the wall with one hand, the other slipping between her legs, finding that spot that just made her crazy, the one he'd been merciless with on the plane to Vegas, when she couldn't make a sound for fear of anyone figuring out what they were doing.

Now, pleasure heated and bloomed inside her. She pulled his hair, called out his name. She was completely his in that moment. He demanded absolute control, absolute surrender. She realized it had been his for the taking all along, whenever he decided to claim it as his own. She just hadn't realized the power he held over her, the things he'd demand.

He finally gave in to her, sinking deep inside her, the feeling exquisite. He froze there for a moment, her body throbbing around his, adjusting, making room, gripping. It just felt so good.

He kissed her again, rocked her body ever so slowly against his with those hands that held her hips. She felt helpless, powerless, breathless, crying out, her body quivering with need.

And soon, it was as if the whole world exploded around them, slipped away, leaving nothing but the two of them, their bodies, their pounding hearts, their mouths, every maddening, adoring, confusing thing she felt for him, swelling up inside her and spilling out, along with the tears seeping out her eyes.

She couldn't do anything but cling to him, lie there weakly against him as his body tensed, he called out her name and sank into her one last time.

When she could still barely move, he slipped away from her, eased her down to stand on her own two feet. Which didn't seem possible, as her legs felt like jelly.

But he stayed close, holding her up with his body, as he shrugged completely out of his shirt, his slacks and underwear, even his socks and shoes. Then he scooped her up into his arms and carried her to his bedroom, laying her on the bed, undressing her himself and tossing the rest of her clothes away one by one.

He was so gorgeous, standing there in the dim light of his room, gloriously naked, those tight hips, narrow waist, powerful thighs, broad shoulders, wicked smile.

"That's what you wanted to do to me in Vegas?" she asked.

'That's just the beginning of what I planned to do with you in Vegas," he told her, then got into the bed beside her and pulled her on top of him.

"Wyatt, I can't," she said. Her legs sprawled onto either side of his hips, her body still warm and wet and throbbing from what he'd already done to her. "I don't have the strength to move."

"You don't have to go far," he said, growing aroused again.

He shifted his hips this way and that, shifted her body, until he was once again inside her, then pulled her down on top of him, so that her breasts pressed against his chest, and took her hips in his hand, showing her what he wanted her to do, until she found the strength to take over the movement herself.

He was so deep inside her this way, and the slightest rocking motion of hers just felt…it felt so good.

"There you go, Jane. You like being in control. Remember?"

She laughed weakly, moaned, thinking there were probably a lot of things she could do to him and thoroughly enjoy, things to experience, to learn, to want, to need. Time to explore, pleasures to seek, to discover.

A moment later, any illusion of control she had had was gone once again. He pulled her hard against him and held her there, surging up and into her, taking what he wanted once more, what she was happy to give.

His fingertips dug into her hips, and she ground herself against him, because being close just wasn't enough. She wanted more, needed it, needed to be a part of him, someone who could never be completely separate from him again.

She fell into the pleasure, limply against him, sated, exhausted, his heart pounding beneath her ear, his body still throbbing with pleasure.

So, she thought, drifting off to sleep, this is what she'd wanted all this time, what had been missing, what had seemed completely out of reach.

No wonder it made people crazy, knowing there was pleasure like this to be had in the world. Now that she knew, what would she do to keep it, to make sure she never lost this with him?

Chapter Fourteen

Wyatt sat at his desk the next day, having gone to the office because he hadn't really known what else to do with himself. He'd woken up late, hadn't even turned on his alarm clock last night.

He'd been too preoccupied to think of anything else.

When he'd woken up, Jane had already been gone, leaving him a note in the kitchen saying she'd gone into the office, that she'd see him later.

So he'd shown up at his office, too, only to have Lucy fuss over him, pouring out sympathy and sadness of her own—she'd been a big fan of Leo—and telling him that surely he didn't need to be here today.

He supposed he could go to Remington Park and clean out Leo's room, if the staff hadn't already done that. He could pick up Leo's things and take them... He didn't know where, didn't want to think of that.

There was the will to probate. He could get started on that, but again, really didn't want to. He was putting off the exes as long as he could, and he was just all out of sorts, unsettled, lost.

Lucy walked in, took one look at him gazing out the window, obviously not doing anything, and said, "Go home."

"I don't want to go home," he said.

"Why not?"

"Because… Jane might be there."

Lucy gave him a funny look. "I thought you liked Jane. I like Jane. I like her a lot."

"Of course I like Jane," he said. "I just… Well… I think she might think we're living together."

That took Lucy by complete surprise. "You let her move in? You actually let a woman move in with you? Wyatt, you don't live with women. It's one of your absolute rules."

"I know. I remember. It's just…" He shrugged. What was there to say? "It's Jane."

"So, she just barged in with her things—"

"No things. Just her. And the clothes she brought back from Las Vegas, the ones her grandmother and Gladdy bought her. She looks so sexy in those things."

Lucy sat down in the big, cushy leather chair opposite his desk. Clearly she thought this was going to take a while. "You're saying, the two of you have just been together since you got back from Vegas?"

"Since we went to Vegas," he said. "Four… Is it four? Yeah. Four days. And nights."

"But, you never invited her to live with you? She just—"

"Arranged a single room for us in Vegas, and then when we got back, came home with me. She's been there ever since."

"Did you give her a key?"

"No," he said.

"Did you ask her to stay?"

"No." She just stayed, taking care of him, not wanting him to be alone. Wyatt frowned.

"So, she feels bad that you lost Leo, and she's giving you sympathy sex," Lucy figured out, looking pleased with her deduction.

"Well…yeah. I mean, not just that, but…yeah."

"I bet you've never had to resort to sympathy sex in your life, Wyatt. So it's not surprising you wouldn't understand it."

"No. I really don't understand it," he confessed, hoping Lucy could explain. She loved setting him straight on things he supposedly didn't understand about women, loved reminding him he didn't know everything about the opposite sex, no matter how sure he was that he did.

So maybe she could make sense of this. Mostly, how much he liked it, even if it was sympathy sex. Because it felt…just…like…way more than he ever wanted to feel…about anything. But he liked it, and he sure didn't want to give it up.

He wanted sympathy sex and every other kind of sex there was with Jane. It was just… Did she think they were living together now? Was she going to be there, whenever he got home? In his bed every night, until he asked her to leave?

And could he just ask her to leave? He certainly didn't want to hurt her, and he didn't want anyone else to ever hurt her, either. She was Jane. She was sweet and kind and funny and adorable.

"Okay, here it is," Lucy said. "She feels bad for you. She

likes you. She wants you to feel better, so she gives you sympathy sex."

"I don't think Jane does that," he guessed. That's the part that puzzled him, worried him, gave him an added little thrill at having her in his bed. He doubted Jane had ever given anyone sympathy sex in her life.

"You just said she'd been doing it with you for the last four nights," Lucy reminded him.

"Yeah, but…"

"Wyatt, are you trying to tell me it's different with Jane? That she's different, and that what you have is more?"

"I don't know. How am I supposed to know that?"

Lucy was laughing at him. Not to his face, but he could tell, inside she was laughing. She often did that, too.

"What?" he asked.

"Is she going to be there when you get home today?"

"She said she was."

"Okay, but here's the real question. Do you want her to be there when you get home today?"

"I guess, I've gotten used to having her around." There, he'd admitted it.

"Her, or the sex?"

"Both, I guess."

"You should think about that," Lucy advised. "And I think you're actually going to have to talk to her about this. You do talk every now and then, don't you?"

"Yes."

"But if you do decide to talk to her about this, you can't just ask her what she wants or whether she thinks you're living together. You have to be ready to tell her what you want. Do you have any idea what you want?"

Jane, he thought. *Just Jane.*

The way they were now. Nothing more, nothing less. Just this. Jane in his bed, Jane in his apartment. Sweet, generous, sexy Jane.

"Wow," Lucy said, when he didn't say a word. "We're in brand-new territory here, aren't we?"

Wyatt let himself welcome Jane back into his home that evening. They ate the take-out dinner she'd brought with her, and then hustled off to bed once again. He did his absolute best to make sure she wasn't thinking about how sorry she was for him while they were there. And then, when she was curled up naked and sated by his side, he finally said what he had to say.

"Jane, what are we doing?"

"Sleeping. Wyatt, I have to sleep sometimes."

"I know, but… I mean, us, here, together. What are we doing?"

"Nothing for you to get nervous about," she reassured him.

"Are we…living together?" he asked.

"No. I don't do that. I always tell women they're asking for trouble when they drift into a situation like that, with nothing spelled out up front, no clear expectations, no promises, no agreements. Women have absolutely no protection that way, no security. It's a terrible idea. I would never do that. You don't do that, either. Do you?"

"No. I don't."

"There. See? Neither one of us does that. So we're definitely not living together. We're just…spending some time together. For now. Because things are still hard and people shouldn't be alone in hard times. They should have someone with them, someone to help them."

"And when things…aren't so hard? Then what?"

"Then, we'll do something else," she offered. "We'll sit down and talk about it, and we'll decide. On something else."

"Okay," he agreed.

That made sense. Perfect sense. Jane was such a sensible woman. And it meant they didn't have to decide on anything right then, and they could still keep doing this, Jane here with him, in his bed.

That was perfect for now.

Jane could no longer deny it.

She was in trouble.

And when she was in trouble, she went to Gram and Gladdy. She didn't want to, because Gram had just lost Leo, and even though the relationship was incredibly brief, the man hadn't even been dead for a week, and Gram was in mourning. Maybe Gladdy, too. Jane still didn't understand that whole relationship, except that both women seemed as close as ever, and neither one seemed mad at the other.

How could that be?

If Jane found out Wyatt was seeing someone else, she'd be devastated. She might even resort to violence again, and this time, she wouldn't pull her punches at the last minute, like she had with Leo.

Poor Leo.

If he had truly loved Gram, only to have so little time with her… That would be awful, terrible and so unfair. Why would anyone find someone like that, only to lose him hours after marrying her? It seemed too cruel to even contemplate. If he'd loved her. If the Gray men were even capable of that particular emotion.

Jane got to Gram and Gladdy's cottage. Amy was there at work in the kitchen. She dropped what she was doing and came over to give Jane a big hug.

"It's just so awful," Amy said. "Max is devastated. He's never known anyone who died. I didn't even know he knew Mr. Gray that well, but I guess they'd talked a few times, when Max was with your grandmother or Gladdy, and Max really liked him. And your poor grandmother. She's trying to be so brave, but… I think she really loved him, Jane."

Jane agreed. "I think she must have."

"We cleaned out his room the other day. Your grandmother and Gladdy wanted to do it themselves, but I thought they should have help, so I went, too."

"Thank you, Amy. I should have thought of that myself—his room. I would have helped them."

"It's okay. It was hard, but we got it done. We stored his personal belongings in some boxes in your grandmother's closet. She was hoping you could take them to his nephew."

"Of course," Jane agreed. "I'll do that when I leave today."

Amy said she had to get back to the kitchen. "I'm making raspberry lemon bars. They were Mr. Gray's favorite. You should take some home with you. I've been baking way too much lately. I always bake when I'm sad."

Jane said she would take some lemon bars to Wyatt, then went to find her grandmother and Gladdy. They were in Gram's room, tending to a box in the middle of the floor. Gram was holding up a photo, gazing at it lovingly and adding it to a stack of other things spread out across her bed.

Both women looked up when she came in. She hugged

them tightly, thinking she might never get enough of being close to them this way, especially when faced with the possibility of losing them one day, as Wyatt had lost Leo. Gram wouldn't let Jane go, when Jane would have slipped away from her hug. She took both of Jane's hands in hers and held on.

"Darling, you look like you have something on your mind. Like you need your Gram and Gladdy." She tugged her over to the couch. "Come sit and tell us all about it."

Jane sat between the two women, smiled, took a breath and tried for all the world to play it off like it was nothing, when what she really wanted to do was burst into tears.

"I think," she began. "Well, I'm afraid…maybe… probably…that I'm in love with Wyatt."

And then she did burst into tears.

They fussed over her, held her, patted her back, wiped away her tears, put determined smiles on their faces, which was something they always did, even when life seemed to be most bleak. And she was glad for their comfort, their concern and to have them close now, to still have them in her life. But none of it really changed things.

"I promised myself I wouldn't fall for him," she said. "I promised, and I don't know how it happened. He was just here, and he was nice and so sweet to his uncle. He took care of Leo the way I…well, the way I hope I take care of you both."

"You do, darling," Gram said.

"Of course you do," Gladdy added.

"And he seemed so smart and reasonable and gorgeous and sexy, and it was like the whole thing just sneaked up on me, when I wasn't looking. One minute, we were chasing the three of you to Vegas, and the next, Leo was dying. Wyatt was devastated. Just lost and so sad and alone. I couldn't stand it. I had to help him. I just couldn't leave him like that. And so I…"

"Comforted him?" Gladdy guessed.

"Yes. I did. I mean, I didn't set out to do that, but then… I had to. I had to do something. And not just something. I would have done anything to try to make him feel better, because my heart was breaking for him. I just couldn't leave him. I still haven't left him, not since it happened. I don't think I can."

"You're living together?" Gram asked, while Jane took a breath, finally.

"No. I don't do that. That's really not a good idea. Nothing spelled out, nothing agreed upon, nothing to keep you from getting hurt when things go wrong, and they always go wrong, eventually. But it's…it's…" Jane started bawling again. "Okay, yes, I am. I'm living with him, even through I swore to him that we're not, because I don't do that. And he doesn't do that, either."

Gladdy frowned. "Jane, darling, you're either living with the man or not. I'm not asking a philosophical question."

"Yes, I'm there. With him. I've been with him since we got to Vegas that first night. I knew it wasn't the smartest thing to do, once I got scared and really thought about it. Because we haven't talked about anything—except that we swear we're not living together, which I know is ridiculous, believe me. But we actually said that. We claimed we aren't living together, and yet, we are. It's such a bad idea. I know that. I teach women that all the time. It's just…when it came right down to it, even knowing that, I couldn't leave him alone."

Jane had to stop to breathe and to wipe her eyes with the tissue Gladdy handed her. It was all so awful.

"Gladdy, none of it seemed as important as Wyatt not being alone. He was more important to me than being smart and protecting myself."

"Oh, Jane!" they said together, beaming at her in unison, looking as if she'd given them the world.

"You love him," Gram said.

"Yes, obviously, you do," Gladdy agreed. "This is so wonderful!"

"No, it's not!" she told them. "He doesn't love me! He's just sad and lonely and hurting, and I'm…I'm…I'm afraid that to him, being with me is better than being alone right now."

And then she sobbed some more, not even trying to stop.

"It looks like I'm truly one of the Carlton women after all," Jane cried. "I've fallen in love with a man who's going to break my heart. I know he is."

Wyatt went shopping after work. He normally left this sort of thing—buying presents for women—to Lucy, who had excellent taste. But this he wanted to pick out himself. This was for Jane.

He'd decided she couldn't possibly look any better than she did in a lace camisole, those perfect, small breasts of hers cupped so delicately in the thin satin and lace that hugged her body, covering her but not really covering her. His heart started thudding just thinking about how she looked, how she felt, in those things. And he wanted her to have more of them. Plus, he figured what he bought her, he'd get to take off her, so this was a classic win-win situation.

And it was just lingerie, nothing outrageously expensive, nothing he thought Jane would object to a man purchasing for her. He felt perfectly safe giving her this, and he very much wanted to give her something, some little thing, when she'd given him so much.

So he went to the lingerie store, coming out with a huge black box with a fancy gold ribbon on it, maybe going a tad overboard. But it was for Jane.

He put it on the coffee table back at his apartment, so she'd see it as soon as she came in and sat down, and then waited none-too-patiently.

Where was she?

It was almost seven. She was always here before seven, usually by six. Neither one of them had been working long hours this week.

He felt a little uneasy.

She was coming here, wasn't she? Even if they weren't living together? She wouldn't just *not* show up here without telling him. Would she? Because it wasn't as if they had any kind of agreement about these things, but still… It was Jane. She wouldn't desert him without a word.

Hard as it was to admit, he trusted her. He was starting to count on her, to enjoy knowing that when he got home at night, she would be waiting, or if not, that she would be there soon.

Wyatt drummed his fingertips on the coffee table, right next to the big black box of lingerie, looking at the clock once again, fighting the urge to pace.

He was being ridiculous. He knew it.

She was fine. Everything was fine, and she'd be here any minute. He was worrying about nothing. Old habits, and all. His mother had walked out on him and his father without a word one day. The only stepmother he'd ever let himself get close to had done the same thing. His own father had often walked out the same way, and Wyatt had always ended up with Leo. Leo had been there for him and now Leo was gone.

It didn't mean Jane would go anywhere. Intellectually, he knew that. But old habits died hard. That feeling—of expecting people to just disappear, to be the same as every other person in his life had been—seemed to have a life of its own inside of him.

God, he hated this. Hated it.

He finally heard her at the door at seven-fifteen, pulling it open before she could, telling himself he was being ridiculous, telling himself, of course, she was here, and she was fine.

Except…she wasn't.

Clearly, she'd been crying. Her face was splotchy, her eyes red-rimmed.

"Jane?" He grabbed her hands the moment she set her car keys and her briefcase down on the floor. "What's wrong?"

"Nothing." She sniffled. "I went to see Gram and Gladdy. That's all."

"What's wrong with them?" He'd come to adore them himself, couldn't stand the idea that anything had happened to them.

"Nothing. We just…we talked, that's all. They'd sorted through Leo's room the other day, and Gram sent some of those things with me for you. She said she's kept a few photos, and that she'll have copies made and get the originals to you soon, if that's okay."

"That's fine," he said.

"And she kept his cologne. It smells like him. She loved the way he smelled."

© 2009 HARLEQUIN ENTERPRISES LIMITED ® and ™ are trademarks owned and used by the trademark owner and/or its licensee. Printed in the U.S.A.

I accept your offer!

Please send me two free *Silhouette Special Edition®* novels and two mystery gifts (gifts worth about $10). I understand that these books are completely free—even the shipping and handling will be paid—and I am under no obligation to purchase anything, ever, as explained on the back of this card.

About how many NEW paperback fiction books have you purchased in the past 3 months?

❏ 0-2   ❏ 3-6   ❏ 7 or more
E4LM   **E4LX**   **E4MA**

235/335 SDL

Please Print

FIRST NAME

LAST NAME

ADDRESS

APT.#   CITY

STATE/PROV.   ZIP/POSTAL CODE

**Visit us online at
www.ReaderService.com**

▶ Detach card and mail today. No stamp needed.

The Reader Service—Here's how it works: Accepting your 2 free books and 2 free gifts (gifts valued at approximately $10.00) places you under no obligation to buy anything. You may keep the books and gifts and return the shipping statement marked "cancel". If you do not cancel, about a month later we'll send you 6 additional books and bill you just $4.24 each in the U.S. or $4.99 each in Canada. That is a savings of 15% off the cover price. It's quite a bargain! Shipping and handling is just 50¢ per book in the U.S. and 75¢ per book in Canada.* You may cancel at any time, but if you choose to continue, every month we'll send you 6 more books, which you may either purchase at the discount price or return to us and cancel your subscription.
*Terms and prices subject to change without notice. Prices do not include applicable taxes. Sales tax applicable in N.Y. Canadian residents will be charged applicable provincial taxes and GST. Offer not valid in Quebec. Credit or debit balances in a customer's account(s) may be offset by any other outstanding balance owed by or to the customer. Please allow 4 to 6 weeks for delivery. Offer available while quantities last. All orders subject to approval.

▼ If offer card is missing write to: The Reader Service, P.O. Box 1867, Buffalo, NY 14240-1867 or visit www.ReaderService.com

BUSINESS REPLY MAIL
FIRST-CLASS MAIL   PERMIT NO. 717   BUFFALO, NY

POSTAGE WILL BE PAID BY ADDRESSEE

THE READER SERVICE
PO BOX 1867
BUFFALO NY 14240-9952

NO POSTAGE
NECESSARY
IF MAILED
IN THE
UNITED STATES

"She can have anything she wants," he stated, still not thinking he was getting the whole story here.

Something was wrong. Why would Jane be upset by anything from Leo's room?

"The first box is just outside the door. I put it down to let myself in."

"I'll get it."

He did, looking at the thing as if something in it might jump out and bite him. It was just a box. Photos of the exes, Wyatt saw, one of him and Leo, one of him and Leo and his father, a few books and some papers.

He'd forgotten about the box he'd brought home, about Jane's present, until she walked into the living room and saw it. He set Leo's things down on the floor by the sofa and then took a seat beside Jane, happy to have something here that he hoped would make her happy, too.

"I got you a present today," he declared.

She sat there, looking surprised and a little apprehensive.

Why would the idea of him bringing her a present leave her uneasy?

He had that tight feeling in his throat again, not the full-blown, awful choking feeling, but something that seemed as if it might turn into that.

"Go ahead," he spoke, while he still could. "Open it."

She smiled, but only with her mouth, not with her eyes, and untied the big gold ribbon, pulling it off the top of the box. Inside were a half-dozen camisoles with matching lacy panties and silk robes of different colors.

"I had trouble making up my mind. So I got all of them," he said, thinking, too late, that he might have done something wrong.

She laughed, barely, and he thought he saw a hint of tears in her eyes, as she reached out and ran her hand along the pale yellow set. "They're beautiful."

"One for every day of the week except Sunday. I thought on Sunday, you could just be naked, all day," he tried, seeing if that would win him a real smile.

No luck.

"Pick a color. See if they fit," he said.

And the minute she did and disappeared into the bathroom in the master bedroom, he started digging through that box of Leo's things, needing to know what the hell was going on.

Chapter Fifteen

There was nothing in the box to bring anyone to tears.

Not that he saw, looking through it quickly.

Photos. Lots of photos. Leo's diplomas from both college and grad school. Marriage licenses. Divorce decrees. Various financial records. An envelope from a lawyer with a Las Vegas address, marked Prenuptial Agreement.

Wyatt didn't think the prenup could have upset her. She already knew Leo and Kathleen had signed one. She'd even wanted her grandmother to have one to protect Kathleen's own assets, so Jane couldn't have been surprised Leo would have wanted one to protect himself, too.

Wyatt opened the big envelope. He was executor of Leo's estate, after all, and he didn't see anything else that might upset anyone in this box.

He pulled out copies of a prenup, standard stuff, both keeping assets they had brought into the marriage, making no claim on the other's assets, agreeing to divide equally any assets they had acquired during the course of the marriage.

Nothing there to be upset about.

The next stack of papers said… Last Will and Testament of Leonardo Thomas Gray, dated the same day as the prenups, the day he and Kathleen went to Las Vegas and got married.

Leo made a new will?

Wyatt sat down, surprised.

He'd drawn up all of Leo's various wills, handled all of his divorces since Wyatt had passed the bar, done all of his prenups. Why would Leo ever make a new will without Wyatt?

He glanced at the cover letter accompanying the will….

Dear Mr. Gray,
Believe I've covered all the changes you asked for…keeping all previous bequests from the most recent will…adding $5,000 in trust for Maxwell Carson, $20,000 for new weight-room equipment at Remington Park and $500,000 in trust for Margaret Jane Carlton….

Leo left Jane a half-million dollars?

That was impossible.

The bathroom door opened and Jane walked out, wrapped in pale yellow silk that fell from her shoulders down to the floor, a hint of the matching lace camisole showing between the folds of the robe.

No wonder she looked so apprehensive when she came home.

He was about to figure out the scheme. That her grand-mother and Gladdy hadn't wanted Leo's money. That part was true. They'd gotten it for Jane instead.

"Margaret Jane Carlton?" he asked.

"What?"

She played innocent, and did it very well, he saw, in-furiating him all the more. "Is your full name Margaret Jane Carlton?"

"Yes. Wyatt, what's wrong?"

Oh, God, she was really good at it. All innocent and treacherously beautiful and infuriating. He didn't think a woman had ever hurt him as much as she just had.

"I found out about the money, Jane. But then, you knew I was about to. You brought the box with the new will in it. That's why you were so upset when you walked in. Dreading this little scene?"

"What scene? What money? Wyatt, what are you talking about?" she asked, walking toward him.

"The money!" he roared, taking some measure of sat-isfaction in seeing her jump, startled, stopping in her tracks when he said it.

"What money?" she whispered.

"Leo's money! The half-million dollars you got him to leave you!"

She shook her head. "Why would Leo ever leave me half-a-million dollars?"

"Careful manipulation by three greedy, scheming wom-en, I'd guess."

She took that like a blow, wavering on her feet and clutching the ends of the robe together. "You think my grandmother, Gladdy and I tricked Leo out of a half-million dollars?"

"I know you did. I'm reading his new will. It's all right here in black and white." He smacked the papers against the frame of the door leading to the bedroom.

"You're crazy," she insisted.

"It's right here, Jane! You can't play innocent anymore! God, I should have known all along. I grew up with women like you. My entire life, I saw nothing but women like you, out for all they could get from my father and Leo, even from me. I can't believe this. I can't believe I was this stupid! I was actually starting to trust you, to count on you. I even told someone this week that you were different from the other women I've known." He shook his head, laughed bitterly. "What a crock."

"Wyatt, I have no idea what you're talking about—"

"God, I have no patience for this. Just get out!" he yelled, and when she didn't move, kept right on yelling. "Get out or so help me, God, I will throw you out."

She still didn't budge, just stood there, gaping at him.

He started toward her, angrier than he'd ever been in his life, and she edged away, backing around the perimeter of the room and toward the front door.

"Wyatt, please," she begged.

"None of it was real?" He could still hardly believe it. "None of it?"

"Of course it was. All of it was real!"

"Get out!" he roared.

She grabbed her keys, left there by the door, didn't bother with shoes or clothes or anything else, and fled.

He picked up the nearest thing he could reach, a vase of some kind, and threw it, feeling some sense of satisfaction as it shattered against the front door she'd just slammed shut as she escaped.

* * *

Jane didn't have on any shoes.

She was shaking all over, trying to hold the robe together. She had her car keys, thank goodness, but no shoes.

Walking hurt. The asphalt was grainy, lumpy, and here and there were little pebbles that she stepped on.

It hurt.

But not as much as her heart.

She was still sobbing. One couple passed her and looked scared of her, and another kindhearted older woman asked if she needed help, the police or an ambulance or something. She thanked her and swore she was okay, which was a complete lie, but she just wanted to get away, to get someplace where she could be alone and cry in private, no one looking at her, no one wondering what was wrong.

Why in the world would Leo Gray leave her all that money? She hadn't even liked him, and he'd hardly known her.

Vaguely, she considered that Gram might have asked him to leave Jane some money, but surely Gram knew that Jane was incredibly responsible with money and well on her way to being completely financially secure. She wasn't wealthy, but she earned a good living and had always had a knack for investments that turned out well. She'd been investing in the stock market since she was twelve.

So this didn't make any sense.

And how could Wyatt believe this whole time that she'd been out for nothing but money? That she and her sweet Gram and Gladdy had schemed to get their hands on Leo's money?

She sobbed so hard she dropped her keys, and then

while she wasn't paying attention, she stepped on something that really hurt. At least, she'd made it to her car. She hobbled, mostly on one foot, to the door and got in, her need to just sit there and cry it out warring with her need to get away from here, away from Wyatt.

Wanting to get away won. She dried her tears as best she could, though more fell right away to replace them. Then she headed for her apartment and the blessed solitude to be found there.

It was late before Jane stopped crying, and her brain worked well enough to want to think, logically, about what might have happened. And then, she just couldn't leave all the questions until morning.

She called Gram, apologizing profusely for waking her and likely scaring her. Any phone call at this hour was almost always about something bad.

"Gram, you didn't ask Leo to leave me some money, did you?" she asked, her voice raw from all the crying.

"Jane, darling, what in the world is wrong? What's happened? You sound awful. Are you sick?"

"No. I've just... Wyatt and I had a fight," she admitted, then started to cry again, mad at herself for doing it but unable to stop.

"About what? What did that man do to you?"

"Threw me out of his apartment—"

"Told you to get out? Or actually threw you out, because if he hurt you, Gladdy and I will—"

"Just told me to get out," she rushed on. "Sorry."

"Jane, honey, you're crying your eyes out? Over a man?"

"Yes," she confessed. "Gram, you have to tell me. Did you ask Leo to leave me money in his will?"

"No. Of course not. Why would I? You're doing fine. Aren't you?"

"Yes," she said.

"I never imagined you needed any money from me or Gladdy, and I certainly knew you'd be insulted at the idea of any man giving you money."

"Yes, I would. But Wyatt says he did. He said Leo made a new will in Las Vegas, and he left me a half-million dollars, left some money to Remington Park for a weight room—"

"Now, he did talk about the weight room. That it just wasn't what it should be. Apparently, he liked to lift weights."

"Okay, so that part makes sense. And there was one other thing. $5,000 to someone named…Maxwell. I don't know any Maxwell. Do you? Maxwell Carson, I think."

"That's Amy's last name. Carson. Her son's name is Max. Yes, I bet that's Max. Leo adored him."

"Enough for Leo to leave Max money in his will?"

"Maybe. We kept Max one day, when he had a day off from kindergarten and Amy's babysitter canceled at the last minute. Leo had so much fun with Max. He said it was a shame, how hard Amy worked for so little money, and he worried about her being able to take care of Max."

"Okay, so that makes sense, I guess. But what about me? Why me? He wouldn't just leave me that much money. Would he?"

"I don't know," Gram said. "I'll think about it while Gladdy and I get a cab and come see you."

"No, it's late, and I'm fine—"

"You are most certainly not fine. We'll call a cab. We'll be there in thirty minutes. No arguments. We're taking care of you now."

They arrived in less time than that, letting themselves in with their key, and rushed into Jane's bedroom, fussing and hugging her close and trying to dry her tears, as if she was a little girl again.

It felt so nice, Jane decided. She hardly ever got fussed over, hardly ever allowed it.

"That horrible man!" Gladdy said. "Throwing you out of his apartment? Breaking your poor, dear heart? How dare he?"

She was incensed on Jane's behalf, ready to do battle if necessary, maybe even eager for it, and just knowing that made Jane feel better. They sat on the bed with her, one of them on either side, snuggling close, the three Carlton women, together through good times and bad.

She absolutely adored them.

Gram went to the kitchen eventually, insisting ice cream was in order, that it helped soothe all heartaches, and then nearly had a fit when she found a little blood on Jane's kitchen floor.

"What did that man do to you?" she demanded, looking fierce.

"He didn't hurt me. I told you that. I just… I left his apartment without my shoes, and when I was walking to my car, I stepped on something. I didn't even realize I'd cut my foot until I got back here. I thought I'd wiped all the blood up, but I guess I missed some."

"Let me see what he did! Let me see right now," Gram demanded.

Jane pulled the covers off her foot, which she'd bandaged, hastily and not very well before she'd climbed into her bed. Gram and Gladdy fussed some more, unwrapping it, moving a lamp so they could see it more clearly, then insisting that the cut was deep and might well need stitches.

"It does not. I just stepped on something—"

"Glass, most likely. And if it is glass, it could still be in there, and it has to come out."

"Gram, I just want to sleep, honestly. I feel so much better that both of you are here, but now, I'm just exhausted."

Gram frowned, but didn't argue. "Okay, but I'm not leaving you."

"Me either," said Gladdy. "We'll have a sleepover. We haven't done that in a long time. It'll be fun. We'll see how your foot is in the morning. And decide what we're going to do with that awful man. He's not going to get away with treating you like this. We won't let him."

Wyatt drank himself into oblivion that night.

It was the only thing that made him not really feel anything, and he needed desperately to not feel anything. Because mostly, he just felt way too much.

Feelings, he thought, snarling. Who needed to feel anything, really? It was all so…messy and upsetting and just came out of nowhere at a man. One minute, he was going along with his life, just fine, and the next… He was flat on the floor, drunk and wishing he couldn't feel a thing.

Life had to be easier that way.

He'd been just fine until Jane came along. Beautiful, deceitful, lying Jane.

He'd actually thought she was different and had even told her so. That was the most infuriating part. He'd believed her. About everything.

What an idiot he was!

He woke sometime later—in daylight as he could see from the windows of his apartment—to someone pounding on his door. Or was that the pounding in his head? Maybe both, he decided.

Even sitting up, slowly and carefully, the room still did that sickening tilt. And the pounding on the door kept right on going. He wasn't imagining it. It wasn't all in his head.

He finally got to the door, opened it, and Jane's grandmother, who'd worked herself into a full-blown rage, swept inside, looking at him as if he was the devil himself.

Wyatt fought the urge to shield himself from her, thinking she might literally attack at any moment. She fumed at him, bringing her hands up as if she was weighing the value of a good, quick punch or two.

He told himself that surely he could duck the punch of a little old lady, if he had to and stood his ground. He just wished the room would stop its sickening tilt every time he turned his head. He wasn't sure he could duck a punch when the room wasn't even standing still.

"You stupid boy!" she said.

"And you," he shot back. "Ms. I Don't Need Leo Gray's Money. He was dying, and the last days he spent on this earth, he spent with you. You and your granddaughter taking him for half-a-million dollars!"

"I didn't take anything from him!"

"No, you left that part to Jane. What a great scam. I can just hear you, working it on Leo. 'It's not for me, Leo. I don't need anything for myself. But Jane…poor Jane, I worry about her so—"

"Only when it comes to men, not money. Is your view of women so twisted that you can't even fathom the existence of a woman who earns her own money? Is smart and sensible and financially secure on her own? That there might be at least one or two women in this world who didn't want the Gray men for their money?"

"Haven't found one yet," Wyatt retorted.

"Yes, you have. You stupid boy! Where is this will? I want to see it for myself, because I don't believe Leo would have done this. He would have known the quickest way to ruin anything between you and Jane would be for you to think she was after your money. Or his."

"And why would he be so worried about ruining anything between me and Jane?"

"Because this whole thing was a setup. This whole thing between me and Leo and Gladdy, all the trouble we caused. It was us trying to get you and Jane together."

Wyatt laughed. "Oh, please. I don't have any trouble getting women. Leo knows that."

"Not any woman you'd ever want to keep. He knew that very well." She fumed at him, then threw up her hands as if to surrender. "He was dying, Wyatt. Think about it. He knew he was dying, and he said the only regret he had about his life was that he was leaving you so suspicious of women that you might never truly trust one. He couldn't stand the idea of being gone, and you being left all alone."

"Leo knows I can take care of myself—"

"Of course. He just didn't want you to have to do that. He said your father's lousy and always has been, that your mother ran off when you were little, and that he's been the only constant in your life. He loved you like a son, said he always thought you should have been his, and he spent his last days here on earth seeing that you'd be taken care of after he was gone, that you'd have someone to love you."

"And this person I need so much in my life, this great love of mine, is Jane?" He almost choked on the words, but he got them out. "Give-me-half-a-million-and-I'll-love-you Jane? I could find lots of women who'd swear they would love me for a lot less than that."

"Show me the will. Right now. Did you even read the whole thing?" she demanded.

"I read enough—"

"We'll see about that. Give it to me!"

He found the damn thing and shoved it at her.

Him and Jane? Someone to love him once Leo was gone?

Leo knew you couldn't buy love. He'd tried his whole life, and it had never worked. He knew better than anybody.

So did Wyatt.

Chapter Sixteen

"Oh, my God!," Kathleen said a moment later. "This is what you're so upset about? I thought it might be this. It was the only thing I could imagine Leo doing. You object to Jane helping poor women get some kind of education or job training with Leo's money? Honestly, Wyatt, that's—"

"What?" He snatched the papers out of her hand. "Poor women getting an education? He left Jane a half-million. You're trying to convince me that she's going to run some kind of charity with Leo's money? You never quit, do you? It's one scam after another—"

"It's right here in black and white. You didn't even read it? You just glanced at this and jumped to the wrong conclusions and broke her heart? You stupid, stupid boy!"

"What?"

"Leo wanted to leave me some of his money. He wanted to make sure Gladdy and I never wanted for anything, and

I had to work hard to convince him that we never would, that Jane had already seen to that. And he felt bad about how he'd treated her, all the trouble we'd caused trying to force the two of you together. I told him Jane didn't want for anything, either, except a man in her life. Although if I'd known you were like this, I never would have gone along with it—"

"Gone along with what?"

"Setting up you and Jane. Leo and Gladdy and I are old, but we're not stupid. We knew if we caused enough trouble or worried you and Jane enough, that you'd likely end up at Remington Park, hopefully working together to sort out our troubles. And it worked beautifully, I might add, until now!"

"You married him," Wyatt reminded her. "You're telling me, you and Leo got married as a scam to throw Jane and me together?"

"No. We never planned to actually get married, but once we got to Vegas, we were so happy. He was just a delight-ful person, and he finally told me that he was ill, that he didn't think he had long to live, and… It's silly, I know. I'm not really a romantic, but… He was so sweet, and I just adored him. We thought, why not? And then, he was gone."

"And conveniently left Jane half-a-million dollars in his new will."

"I didn't know he was making a new will. We did the prenup together, and then I went to pick out a dress. I guess he must have gone back and had the will made up then."

"Right," Wyatt said, not believing a word of it.

"Leo kept wanting to do something for Jane, and I told him the only thing Jane really wanted that required money she didn't have was to be able to help women like Max's mother, Amy. Jane can get women like that loans and grants for tuition, but they still have living expenses, and there are only so many hours a day to work, take care of a child and go to school. She wanted to be able to provide grant money to help. I guess Leo thought that was a good idea and a good use of some of his money. Is that really so awful? Is that a reason to break Jane's heart?"

"It doesn't say anything about money for poor women like Amy," he yelled. "It just says money for Jane. A half-million dollars for Jane!"

"I want you to know, I've never seen her cry like that, never seen her so devastated. And to throw her out of your apartment without even her clothes on, without her shoes. She hurt herself getting out of here, you know. She was bleeding. I told Gladdy to take her to the emergency room this morning, while I came over here to straighten you out!"

Wyatt was scanning the papers, looking for the part about Jane getting all that money, to shut up her grandmother, and started to feel a little uneasy, a little sick to his stomach, when he got to the details of the half-million-dollar trust for Jane.

No, not exactly for Jane. For Jane to administer, but for… Women seeking an education or job training, particularly those with children to support while they went back to school. Like Amy. Leo wanted Amy to be able to go back to school, so she could take better care of herself and Max.

Maxwell Carson, from the will, the $5,000 in a trust for his education.

Leo wanted Amy to be the first recipient of a grant from the half million in trust he'd set up, money for Jane to administer as trustee.

Wyatt closed his eyes, felt the most tremendous sense of relief and utter joy he could imagine.

Jane was Jane, the Jane he'd always thought she was, the Jane he'd always adored.

And he'd been an absolute ass to her last night.

"Oh, my God," he muttered.

Kicked her out, screamed at her, frightened her so much, she hadn't even taken the time to get dressed before she ran away from him.

"I'm an idiot," he said.

"Yes, you are," her grandmother agreed.

"Wait... Did you say something about her getting hurt?"

"Yes, idiot boy!"

"Jane got hurt running out of here?"

"Yes!"

"Hurt how? What happened?" He'd been only half listening while he read the details of the trust. "Did you say something about her in the emergency room?"

Kathleen nodded, looking as if he was a man getting what he deserved right now, and she was happy about that, that no one got away with messing with Jane while she was around to stop it.

"What happened to her? Where is she?" He started looking for his keys. Where the hell were his keys? Where was Jane?

"I'm not sure what hospital they took her to," her grandmother said.

"But what happened? What's wrong with her? How badly was she hurt?"

"They hadn't examined her when I left the E.R. Gladdy stayed with her, and I came to find you, to tell you what an idiot you are!"

He stared at the woman. "We have to find her. We have to find out what's wrong with her. We have to make sure she's okay."

Kathleen just nodded.

And then he saw, he was afraid he saw, just how vengeful the Carlton women could be with a man who dared to hurt one of their own.

"You're not going to help me find her? You're not going to tell me where she is?"

"I'm not sure if she'd want you to know where she is." And then the woman just stood there and glared at him.

"Call Gladdy," he demanded.

"She's not answering her phone," Kathleen claimed. "And she's even madder at you than I am. So I don't think she's going to help you, either."

Wyatt raked a hand through his hair, blinked to try to clear his blood-shot eyes.

Jane was out there somewhere, hurt, heartbroken, crying her eyes out over him, thinking he hated her, knowing he didn't trust her at all.

"I have to find her," he said. "I have to tell her how wrong I was. I have to get her to forgive me."

"Good luck with that," Kathleen said, looking as if she could enjoy torturing him like this for days for daring to hurt her beloved Jane.

He went to three emergency rooms, thinking of all the ways a woman could get hurt running out of an apartment building, begging E.R. clerks to tell him if they had a Jane Carlton there, before he finally started thinking halfway clearly.

Once he did, he knew in his heart that if Jane were

really and truly injured, her grandmother would never have left Jane's side, no matter how mad she was at Wyatt.

So this was just about payback, grandmother-style, and Kathleen was really good at it because he'd been terrified, running around town like a crazy man.

Okay. He forced himself to be still, to breathe. If she wasn't badly injured, she was either at her apartment, with Gladdy at Remington Park or they were hiding her somewhere to torture him some more.

Wyatt frowned, thinking he deserved torture, deserved all sorts of despicable acts against his person. He'd been absolutely awful to Jane. Jane who'd been nothing but kind and generous and tender to him.

He decided he'd start at her townhouse and go from there. He got there and pounded on the door until Gladdy opened it, looking every bit as furious as Kathleen's grandmother had been.

"Is she here?" Wyatt begged.

Gladdy just glared at him.

"Kathleen let me have it. I promise. I've been to three emergency rooms already, searching like a mad man. Gladdy, please? Is she here?"

"Three emergency rooms?" Gladdy asked.

Wyatt nodded. "I think I scared the clerks. I'm probably lucky they didn't try to inject me with something to calm me down and put me on a psych hold. Then it might have been days before I could find Jane. Please, Gladdy. I have to find her."

"She cried all night," Gladdy reiterated. "Over you. Jane's never cried like that over a man. She's never cared that much for a man."

And he was grateful to hear it. Not the tears part, but

the caring part. If she was that upset about what he'd done to her, it had to mean she really cared about him, and if she cared that much, he had to be able to get her to forgive him eventually.

"Gladdy, I'm begging you. Tell me where Jane is."

She just stood there, mute, outraged and without a hint of sympathy for him.

Damn. What was he going to do now?

"Sorry," he said, literally picking her up and setting her to the side, to get around her and into the apartment, calling out as he went. "Jane? Are you here? You have to talk to me! I'm not leaving until you do. Jane?"

Jane heard the commotion. She was afraid half the building heard Gladdy yelling at him, Wyatt begging and insisting he had to find Jane.

She braced herself as best she could, but honestly, how could a woman ever truly prepare herself for the reality of Wyatt Gray in the flesh? The things he did to a woman. The things he made her feel, made her wish for, made her come to count on?

No woman could ever be truly prepared against that, Jane decided.

He found her in her bed, wearing a pair of soft cotton pajamas, her eyes still red from crying, and her foot, bandaged and propped up on a pillow.

"You *are* hurt," he said, looking shocked as he came to sit on the side of the bed and inspected her swaddled foot. "I thought Kathleen had to be lying to me—"

"Because all women lie, right?" Jane shot back.

"No, because she wanted to torture me for what I did to you, and she's really good at it," he said, as if he admired a woman who was good at that. "And I deserve to be tortured. I know that. I've been like a crazy man. She just told me you were hurt leaving my apartment last night, and she wouldn't tell me how. She wouldn't even tell me which emergency room you'd been taken to. I've been all over town."

"Emergency room?" Gram told him that? "Wyatt, I'm fine. I got three stitches from stepping on some glass in the parking lot because I didn't take the time to grab my shoes before I ran out. The only reason we went to the emergency room was because my doctor's out of town, and her office couldn't work me in today. They said I really should have a tetanus shot, to not let it wait."

He put his hand on her foot, holding it through the bandages, as if he still couldn't stand the idea that she'd been hurt. What had Gram done? Made it sound as if she'd run out into the street and been plowed down by a car or something?

Jane felt a teensy bit sorry for him.

"I didn't know anything about the money. I swear," she said, still hurt that he could so easily believe she was just like every other woman he'd ever known. "And I won't take it. I'll just refuse. Leo can't make me take his money."

"No, he wanted you to have it. I'm sure of it now. You should have it."

Oh, God, Jane thought, deciding it still hurt more than she would have thought possible. Was that it? The money but not him? Was that what he was trying to say?

She shouldn't be so surprised. She didn't think he'd ever trusted her anyway. Not after what she'd seen last night. And honestly, who could blame him, the way he'd grown up? She understood. She felt like a fool for ever trusting him, too. For putting aside all the lessons she'd learned in her mixed-up childhood. She'd been so smart about protecting herself. Until she had met him.

"Wyatt, there is no way I'm taking that money. Now, would you please go?" She turned to stare at the window, blinking back tears, mad as could be at the idea of them actually falling and him seeing her cry again.

"No," he said. "I won't. I'm an idiot. I'm a mean-tempered ass. I took the least little bit of information and blew up at you. I let years of experience with women— none of whom were you—ruin something beautiful between us."

"If you hadn't ruined it, something else would have," she admitted.

He moved up on the bed until he was right in front of her, leaned down until even with her head hung low, trying to avoid his gaze, she couldn't.

"My only excuse is that I've never felt like that before, Jane. I never thought I would. Hell, I never wanted to. I'm terrified here. I've never really trusted anybody in my life, except Leo, and he's gone. I can't even talk to him to tell him how terrified I am at the idea of loving you."

"You don't love me," she insisted.

"I think I do. God help me, I do. And I think you love me, too. What are we going to do about that?"

"Ignore it. It'll go away. These things never last," she told him.

"I won't go away. In fact, I'm not leaving here. Just try to throw me out. You and Kathleen and Gladdy, give it your best shot. I'm not going."

"Someone always leaves, Wyatt. We both know that."

"I won't. I meant it. I've never found anyone like you.

As smart and funny and sexy and sweet as you. As delight-
ful as you. As adorable as you. And I'm not leaving."

He sat there like a man taking root, content to wait her
out, to wait out anything.

"This is ridiculous, Wyatt! You apologize to women by
ignoring everything they say and just doing what you want?"

"I'm not leaving."

She felt hot, wet, stupid tears fall down her face then,
and she was so mad she could hardly stand it. Crying! She
was crying! Over a stupid, stubborn man! He looked
panicked at her tears, as if she was fighting dirty or she
might have finally found something to use against him that
might work.

"Please don't do that," he said.

She stared at him, defiant, her tears still falling.

"Jane, come on. You have a strong sense of fairness, and
I'm sure you abhor all sorts of feminine trickery when it
comes to dealing with men. Fight fair here."

"I don't want to fight at all!"

"Well, good. Neither do I. I am so sorry. God, I'm
sorry. I'll never be able to say it enough. I panicked.
That's all there is to it, and I won't do that again, I
swear. And I won't leave you. This man is never going
to leave you, Jane. How can you *not* accept that there
might be one man in the whole entire world who won't
ever leave you?"

"One?" she scoffed. "Just one? And you think you're
it?"

"I know I am."

"It hurts too much, Wyatt," she sobbed, unable to hold
it together at all anymore. God, she hated this! "It's too
hard, too big a risk to take. We both know that. We're both

so sensible. It's one of the first things I liked about you. We both know better than this."

"No, we were wrong, and you know it. Look at Leo. Eighty-six years he had here, most of them as happy as could be, but in the end, what mattered to him? Just the people who loved him. That's it. The rest was just…details. Details and silly things we use to keep score because we're not smart enough to know any better. I can see that now. You can, too, Jane. I know you can."

"No—"

"You were happy with me. I made you happy, I know I did. And I was terrified with you most of the time, terrified of wanting you too much, loving you too much, and losing you. But I'm done with that. I'm here. I love you, and I'm staying. You couldn't make me leave if you tried."

"Gladdy?" she yelled. "Call the police!"

"Go ahead," he dared her. "They'll let me out of jail eventually, and I'll be right back here. I'm the most stubborn man you will ever meet and the most determined."

"The most unreasonable, you mean."

"That, too," he promised, still sitting there.

She heard Gram and Gladdy whispering at the door to her bedroom.

"How's he doing?" Gram asked.

"Better than I expected," Gladdy admitted.

Wyatt grinned hugely. "You know this was all a setup to get us together, don't you?"

"What?"

"Every bit of it," he told her. "Leo couldn't stand the idea of me being alone once he was gone, and he couldn't have found a more generous, kindhearted, loving woman to be by my side. You blew me away, Jane, the way you took care of me, the way you just gave yourself to me, the way you loved me. I'll do the same for you. I promise. Every day of our lives."

"Oh, do you think they'll go to Vegas to get married?" Gladdy asked. "I want to go back to Vegas! What was the name of the chapel?"

"The Love Me Tender Wedding Chapel. Leo would have loved that. Oh, I almost forgot." Gram hurried to Wyatt's side, pulled the huge diamond ring off her finger and handed it to Wyatt. "Leo wanted you to have this. For Jane."

Gram backed out of the room, grinning hugely herself.

Wyatt looked particularly pleased to have a big, sparkly diamond to hold out to her. "See, they've forgiven me, and I adore them both, too. They're going to be the greatest in-laws a man ever had."

"Oh, yes. We will," Gladdy agreed from the doorway.

They were ganging up on her. She couldn't believe it! And Gram and Gladdy were not quick to forgive, not toward anyone who hurt Jane.

"It's a really nice ring," Gram added. "You always said a woman should never refuse good, quality diamonds from a man, Jane."

Jane rolled her eyes, shook her head. Her foot hurt. Her heart hurt.

Wyatt looked as if he'd spent the night in the gutter, passed out drunk, and woken up to some kind of nightmare. She'd never seen him look anything close to awful, and he probably never would. But he looked truly bad right now. Tortured, he'd said. A crazy man who just had to get to her.

"I'm so scared," she whispered.

"So am I, but I'm more scared of being without you," he explained, sounding as honest as a man could be.

If they were both scared, they were at least being honest and at least halfway smart about this, Jane reasoned.

After all, it was an enormous thing, promising your life to someone, to love, honor and cherish, forever.

"I'll sign any kind of prenup you want," Wyatt added. "Just…you know…because I know you'll want one."

"Well, that would be at least one smart thing to do," she admitted.

"And Vegas sounds good," he said. "I have some very fond memories of being in Vegas with you, even with the awful stuff with Leo. We could go back to Vegas."

"We get to go, too, right?" Gladdy asked, sounding delighted. "We want to go!"

"You want to run off right now and get married in Vegas?" Jane couldn't believe it. Just when he was starting to sound reasonable.

"We could even pack this time."

Gram and Gladdy giggled.

"That's crazy, Wyatt."

"I'm a crazy man, Jane. Crazy about you. What do you say? Vegas?"

"It's crazy. He's crazy," she yelled to Gram and Gladdy.

"We'll start packing right now," Gram said.

Wyatt had her hand in his, was sliding the ring on her finger and she wasn't pulling away.

"Marry me," he said. "Love me tender, I'll love you back the same way."

"Wyatt, it's just nuts!"

But by nightfall, he had her on a plane to Vegas, with her panties on this time, but not for long, Wyatt promised.

* * * * *

Harlequin offers a romance for every mood!
See below for a sneak peek from our paranormal
romance line, Silhouette® Nocturne™.
Enjoy a preview of REUNION by USA TODAY
bestselling author Lindsay McKenna.

Aella closed her eyes and sensed a distinct shift, like movement from the world around her to the unseen world.

She opened her eyes. And had a slight shock at the man standing ten feet away. He wasn't just any man. Her heart leaped and pounded. He reminded her of a fierce warrior from an ancient civilization. Incan? She wasn't sure but she felt his deep power and masculinity.

I'm Aella. Are you the guardian of this sacred site? she asked, hoping her telepathy was strong.

Fox's entire body soared with joy. Fox struggled to put his personal pleasure aside.

Greetings, Aella. I'm the assistant guardian to this sacred area. You may call me Fox. How can I be of service to you, Aella? he asked.

I'm searching for a green sphere. A legend says that the Emperor Pachacuti had seven emerald spheres created for the Emerald Key necklace. He had seven of his priestesses and priests travel the world to hide these spheres from evil forces. It is said that when all seven spheres are found, restrung and worn, that Light will return to the Earth. The fourth sphere is here, at your sacred site. Are you aware of it? Aella held her breath. She loved looking at him, especially his sensual mouth. The desire to kiss him came out of nowhere.

Fox was stunned by the request. *I know of the Emerald Key necklace because I served the emperor at the time it was created. However, I did not realize that one of the spheres is here.*

Aella felt sad. Why? Every time she looked at Fox, her heart felt as if it would tear out of her chest. *May I stay in touch with you as I work with this site?* she asked.

Of course. Fox wanted nothing more than to be here with her. To absorb her ephemeral beauty and hear her speak once more.

Aella's spirit lifted. What *was* this strange connection between them? Her curiosity was strong, but she had more pressing matters. In the next few days, Aella knew her life would change forever. How, she had no idea....

Look for REUNION
by USA TODAY *bestselling author Lindsay McKenna,*
available April 2010,
only from Silhouette® Nocturne™.

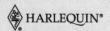

INTRIGUE

WILL THIS REUNITED FAMILY
BE STRONG ENOUGH TO EXPOSE
A LURKING KILLER?

FIND OUT IN THIS ALL-NEW
THRILLING TRILOGY FROM TOP
HARLEQUIN INTRIGUE AUTHOR

B.J. DANIELS

WHITEHORSE
MONTANA

Winchester Ranch

GUN-SHY BRIDE—*April 2010*

HITCHED—*May 2010*

TWELVE-GAUGE GUARDIAN—
June 2010

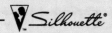

SPECIAL EDITION

INTRODUCING A BRAND-NEW MINISERIES
FROM *USA TODAY* BESTSELLING AUTHOR

KASEY MICHAELS

SECOND-CHANCE BRIDAL

At twenty-eight, widowed single mother
Elizabeth Carstairs thinks she's left love behind
forever....until she meets Will Hollingsbrook.
Her sons' new baseball coach is the handsomest
man she's ever seen—and the more time they
spend together, the more undeniable the
connection between them. But can Elizabeth
leave the past behind and open her heart to
a second chance at love?

FIND OUT IN

SUDDENLY A BRIDE

*Available in April
wherever books are sold.*

HARLEQUIN
Ambassadors

Want to share your passion for reading Harlequin® Books?

Become a Harlequin Ambassador!

Harlequin Ambassadors are a group of passionate and well-connected readers who are willing to share their joy of reading Harlequin® books with family and friends.

You'll be sent all the tools you need to spark great conversation, including free books!

All we ask is that you share the romance with your friends and family!

You'll also be invited to have a say in new book ideas and exchange opinions with women just like you!

To see if you qualify* to be a Harlequin Ambassador, please visit www.HarlequinAmbassadors.com.

*Please note that not everyone who applies to be a Harlequin Ambassador will qualify. For more information please visit www.HarlequinAmbassadors.com.

Thank you for your participation.

HARLEQUIN® *Romance*®

ROMANCE, RIVALRY
AND A FAMILY REUNITED

THE BRIDES
of
BELLA ROSA

William Valentine and his beloved wife, Lucia, live
a beautiful life together, but when his former love Rosa
and the secret family they had together resurface,
an instant rivalry is formed. Can these families
get through the past and come together as one?

Step into the world of Bella Rosa
beginning this April with

Beauty and the Reclusive Prince
by
RAYE MORGAN

Eight volumes to collect and treasure!

www.eHarlequin.com

HARLEQUIN *Presents*

2 Stories in 1

HER MEDITERRANEAN PLAYBOY

Sexy and dangerous—he wants you in his bed!

The sky is blue, the azure sea is crashing
against the golden sand and the sun is hot.

The conditions are perfect for
a scorching Mediterranean seduction
from two irresistible untamed playboys!

Indulge your senses with these two delicious stories

A MISTRESS AT THE ITALIAN'S COMMAND
by *Melanie Milburne*

ITALIAN BOSS, HOUSEKEEPER MISTRESS
by *Kate Hewitt*

Available April 2010 from Harlequin Presents!

www.eHarlequin.com

HP12910

REQUEST YOUR FREE BOOKS!

2 FREE NOVELS PLUS 2 FREE GIFTS!

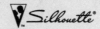

SPECIAL EDITION
Life, Love and Family!

YES! Please send me 2 FREE Silhouette® Special Edition® novels and my 2 FREE gifts (gifts are worth about $10). After receiving them, if I don't wish to receive any more books, I can return the shipping statement marked "cancel." If I don't cancel, I will receive 6 brand-new novels every month and be billed just $4.24 per book in the U.S. or $4.99 per book in Canada. That's a saving of 15% off the cover price! It's quite a bargain! Shipping and handling is just 50¢ per book in the U.S. and 75¢ per book in Canada.* I understand that accepting the 2 free books and gifts places me under no obligation to buy anything. I can always return a shipment and cancel at any time. Even if I never buy another book from Silhouette, the two free books and gifts are mine to keep forever.

235 SDN E4NC   335 SDN E4NN

Name _____ (PLEASE PRINT)

Address _____ Apt. #

City _____ State/Prov. _____ Zip/Postal Code

Signature (if under 18, a parent or guardian must sign)

Mail to the Silhouette Reader Service:
IN U.S.A.: P.O. Box 1867, Buffalo, NY 14240-1867
IN CANADA: P.O. Box 609, Fort Erie, Ontario L2A 5X3

Not valid for current subscribers to Silhouette Special Edition books.

Want to try two free books from another line?
Call 1-800-873-8635 or visit www.morefreebooks.com.